MISS HAYES

MISS WOLFRASTON'S LADIES BOOK 2

JENNY HAMBLY

DEDICATION

To Alanah and William
Always follow your dreams

CHAPTER 1

The drive that led from Miss Wolfraston's Seminary for Young Ladies to the world at large, meandered through a park that was naturalistic in style, and of a not inconsiderable size. The many families, who had been fortunate enough to witness its splendour when delivering their children into the capable hands of Miss Wolfraston, generally considered it to be both elegant and picturesque.

Today, the long, sweeping avenue was crowded with an abundance of carriages, carrying these cherished offspring back into the, no doubt, impatient bosoms of their families, for the summer break. Yet very few of the occupants of these vehicles were of a mind to appreciate the pleasing aspect offered to them, if indeed, they noticed it at all. But then, they had seen it many times before, and so it was perhaps not surprising that the beauty that was so familiar to them, had become dim and indistinct to their dulled senses. It could be the only explanation, for it could hardly be supposed that eagerness to leave the sanctuary of Miss Wolfraston's tender care could cause such a careless lack of attention to their surroundings.

One of the carriages carried two ladies, who, it appeared, were not so remiss. The younger of the two, Miss Charlotte Fletcher, sat very upright, her hands clasped in her lap, and her wide blue eyes fixed firmly on the passing landscape that had marked the boundaries of her life for the past five years. She had become accustomed to thinking of the seminary as her home, and knew every walk and cluster of trees intimately. Her life before she had arrived there had become rather hazy, and so it felt as if she were leaving behind all that was familiar to her, apart from Miss Hayes, her companion on this journey. That lady's presence bolstered her spirits and prevented her from shedding the anxious tears that threatened her composure.

Charlotte had been a very unhappy and withdrawn child when she first arrived at the seminary, after losing both her parents to a putrid fever. Viscount Seymore had been named as her guardian in her father's will. Her cousin had acquired that title on the death of his father, not many months before, but he had numbered only three and twenty years, and did not know what to do with the silent, wisp of a girl. Neither had Miss Wolfraston, at first, and none of the teachers had been able to make her talk or mind her lessons.

Miss Wolfraston had employed Miss Sarah Hayes as a teacher in Charlotte's second term at the school. Sarah had treated the forlorn child with a patience and gentleness that had eventually penetrated her defences. Although only eight years separated them, Charlotte had come to rely on Miss Hayes as she would an aunt, or even a mother.

Sarah was fully aware of this dependency. She'd strived to help Charlotte become more independent, particularly over the last year. Most young ladies left the seminary by their sixteenth year, and so she had been delighted when two other girls Charlotte's age, Lady Georgianna Voss and Miss Marianne Montagu, had arrived. Sarah had ensured they share a room together, hoping that Charlotte might transfer her affections to one or both of them, and develop friendships that might benefit her once she stepped beyond the gates of the seminary and entered society, as she must surely do. Her plan had been at least partially successful. Miss Montagu had readily adopted Charlotte, and even the aloof Lady Georgianna had warmed towards her, in the end.

No one could have been more pleased than Sarah, when Charlotte's Great Aunt Augusta had written to inform her that she had returned from India, and would welcome Charlotte into her own home, Priddleton Hall, near Dorchester. She had not expected to be invited there herself, however. But she had also received a letter summoning her thither. Lord Seymore had mentioned her support to Charlotte, and claiming that she had known Miss Hayes' grandfather, Baron Beaumont, and had met Sarah when she was a child, Lady Carstairs had insisted that she come, for the summer at least, as Charlotte's companion.

This missive had raised conflicting emotions in Sarah's breast. Her first instinct had been to refuse, and indeed, that had been her firm intention. But the bemused, anxious eyes of her protégée had melted her resolve. The affection between them did not lie on Charlotte's side alone. Her heart had gone out to the poor girl as soon as she had learned of her history, for no one knew better than Sarah, how painful it was to have your world turned upside down in an instant.

Although her charge did not realise it, Sarah had been acquainted with Lord Seymore long before she knew Charlotte. Her own mother had died when she was barely out of the nursery and she had developed very close ties of affection with her father. It was not a milky sort of love. Although he had provided her with an extremely accomplished governess, he had treated her very much as if she had been a boy. A keen sportsman, he had raised her to be fearless in the saddle, and had ensured that she could drive a curricle or phaeton as well as any man. He was inordinately proud of both her beauty and her skill, and had not failed to launch her into the *ton* with all the pomp and ceremony he could contrive.

Sarah's auburn hair, creamy complexion, and bewitching green eyes, together with her dauntless spirit, frank ways, and natural grace and elegance, had ensured her success. She had attracted a great many admirers, Lord Seymore amongst them. But although she had found him pleasant enough, he had not captivated her. He had been handsome, certainly, but very young and a little gauche.

It was Lord Turnbull who had caught her eye. He had a knowing air about him, was amusing, and had been an accomplished flirt. He had liked her to cut a dash, and encouraged her to drive her high-perched phaeton in the park, and even allowed her to drive his own curricle, although it was well known that he had paid a small fortune for the showy, matching pair of bays that pulled it. She had easily been able to imagine that her father may have been very like him when he was a young man. Perhaps it was this that had prompted her to accept his offer without very much reflection at all.

Her father had seemed satisfied, but not many weeks later, had met his end in a curricle race. Approaching fifty, he was not as sharp as he had once been. By all accounts, as the race drew near its end, he attempted to overtake his rival on a blind bend. The result had been fatal. The mail coach had been coming in the other direction.

At first, Lord Turnbull had been very supportive of his future wife. But it had slowly emerged to the surprise of all, not least his daughter, that Lord Beaumont had been completely under the hatches. He may have launched his daughter in style, but a series of bad investments, poor management, and a lavish lifestyle, had completely cleaned him out. The rumour that he had purposefully taken such an insane risk on that final bend, began to circulate. In short, the whisper was, that he had all but committed suicide.

The *ton* began to turn its back on her. Although society might have countenanced the boldness and confidence that marked Sarah's character when they thought her wealthy and unmarked by scandal, it did not like to be duped. Even her intended, who had not long before declared himself completely at her feet, turned cold. Lord Turnbull had not protested when she had released him from his obligation.

She had been left bewildered, alone, and without a feather to fly with. She had, at first, been excessively grateful when her father's aunt, Lady Sadler, invited her to live with her as her companion in the depths of the Kent countryside. However, her situation had not been an easy one. Lady Sadler proved to be curmudgeonly and impossible to please. It was also difficult to bear with her frequent, disparaging remarks about her father, or the condescending glances of her many visitors.

The pride and independence that had been

bred into her, had ensured that she eventually rebelled against her subservient situation. She thought it would be better to completely remove herself from the sphere she'd been born into, and so briefly reigned over. She decided that she would rather be paid an honest wage for her labour, rather than live on the crumbs occasionally thrown her way by Lady Sadler. And so, not long after her twentieth birthday, she had found herself at Miss Wolfraston's Seminary for Young Ladies.

Whenever Lord Seymore visited his ward, Sarah played least in sight. Miss Wolfraston had not failed to inform him that Charlotte's improvement was largely down to Miss Hayes' careful handling of the child, and he had claimed that he wished to thank her in person. But she had not wished to be reminded of all that she had lost, or to see the admiration that had once shone so brightly in his eyes, turned to pity, and so she had stubbornly refused. Miss Wolfraston had not pressed her, on the contrary, she had been pleased at such a show of becoming modesty, for even Miss Hayes' work-a-day clothes could not dim her beauty.

Sarah may have, at times, questioned her decision to become a teacher at a school that was so unenlightened as to the education necessary for a young lady, but she had gradually come to terms with her lot over the last five years. It had not been easy however, and now, it seemed that her hard earned equilibrium was to be tested. Although she was reluctant to put herself in a position where she could again become an object of derision or false sympathy, her affection for Charlotte, and her wish to be assured that she was happily settled, had forced her out into the world once more. A wry smile twisted her lips as she acknowledged that a long-hidden part of herself rejoiced at the prospect of leaving behind the stultifying routine of the seminary.

As they at last, passed through the gates of the school, her eyes turned towards her charge.

"Do not look so worried, Charlotte. Judging by the tone of Lady Carstairs' letters, she is very much looking forwards to welcoming you into her home. You are not afraid of her, surely?"

"No, no," Charlotte said quickly. "How can I be when I do not know her? It is only that…"

Sarah smiled gently at her. "Go on, dear."

"Well, what if I do not please her? Great Aunt Augusta is very adventurous you see, and I am not."

"If we were all pleased only by those who reminded us of ourselves, how intolerably conceited we would be! Come, tell me all about her."

Charlotte frowned. "I have been thinking about her a great deal recently, but I know very little really. And I am not sure if what I *think* I remember is accurate, or partly imagined."

"Let us begin with what you do know, then. Lady Carstairs went to India. When?"

"I cannot say exactly when, but it was a few years before I was born, I believe," Charlotte said thoughtfully.

"Let us call it twenty years. Now, why did she go? Was it perhaps because she was connected to somebody who worked for the East India Company?"

A reminiscent smile curled Charlotte's lips. "Now that I can answer. My mother told me the story many times. The short answer is no. She was not. My mother was very proud of Great Aunt Augusta, even though she flouted convention. She always looked forwards to her infrequent letters."

Sarah looked interested. "In what way did she flout convention?"

"She did not at first. She was not a beauty, you see, although my mother thought her very handsome. She said that she was always outspoken. Perhaps that is why she did not take. She eventually became a companion to a Lady Brabacombe, I think. She was a widow. Mama said that she was very crusty, but she cannot have been that dreadful because my aunt stayed with her for fifteen years."

Sarah repressed a shudder. "I admire her fortitude."

Charlotte smiled. "Well, even if it was horrible, it was worth it in the end. When she died, she left my aunt some money. Not a fortune, but enough to make her comfortable. But she did not wish to be comfortable. She wanted an adventure."

"And so she went to India," Sarah said softly. "How marvellous. I think I like her already."

"Yes, she did, alone, apart from a maid. My father was well connected through his years in the navy, and he arranged for her passage when she informed him roundly that she would go whether he helped her or not. It was there she met Lord Carstairs, although he was only Mr Fancot, then. Mama and Papa were very surprised when she wrote to inform them of her marriage for she was well into her thirties. He worked for the supreme court, as a judge. As a matter of fact, until I received my aunt's letter, I was unaware that he had become Lord Carstairs."

"Well, we must be grateful that he has," Sarah said firmly. "For I assume that is the reason he has returned home. I can see no reason for you to be anxious, Charlotte. We know that your aunt was not fond of writing letters, yet she maintained a prolonged, if infrequent, correspondence with your mother. Does this not suggest a fondness on her part for your mama?"

"Yes, I suppose it does," Charlotte admitted. "She did call her *my dear departed niece* in her letter."

"Precisely. Then is it not also reasonable to suppose that she might extend this fondness to her daughter?"

A tentative smile curved Charlotte's lips. "You are right, of course."

"Then stop being such a worrywart, and be prepared to enjoy this new adventure."

They broke their journey at The Red Lion Inn at Shaftesbury. Lady Carstairs had not failed to bespeak rooms and a private parlour for their use. Sarah was very grateful for this forethought for, judging by the noise issuing from the coffee room, the inn was very busy. The maid who showed them to their rooms, confirmed it.

"We're fit to bursting, ma'am. It's the Blandford races. Every inn for miles around is as full as it can hold."

She led them up the stairs and down a long, dim corridor, before pausing in front of a door. She opened it and offered a perfunctory curtsy. "This is your room, miss, and the young lady's is next door." She dropped her voice, leaned towards Sarah, and said, "Your private sitting room is directly opposite the coffee room, miss. I'd steer clear of all the public rooms today if I were you; there's already more than one gentleman downstairs who is a bit on the go, if you get my meaning."

"I think I understand you," Sarah said calmly. "Thank you for the warning."

Her room was clean and comfortable. Its only disadvantage was its situation. It appeared to be directly above the coffee room, and although the ceiling that separated the two rooms managed to muffle the revelry below, it could not completely eliminate the murmur of voices, or the sudden shouts of laughter that would rise above them at regular intervals. She sighed. It would be useless to request another room when there was clearly none to be had.

She suggested to Charlotte that they take a stroll around the small market town. It was set atop a hill, and the only remarkable thing about

it was the breathtaking views over the sur-
rounding countryside. As it was far too hot to
attempt to walk down any of the steep cobbled
lanes, they soon returned to the inn to take their
dinner.

The carpet in the parlour was a trifle threadbare, and the furniture somewhat rudimentary,
however, the food was surprisingly good.

The walk seemed to have done Charlotte
good. There was a delicate pink bloom in her
cheeks, and the tension seemed to have gone
from her.

"I like this," she said softly.

"Yes, the chicken is very good," Sarah
agreed.

Charlotte laughed. "I do not mean the food,
Miss Hayes, I meant this…" She waved her
hand back and forth between them. "Us, eating
a meal together, alone. I believe I could quite
easily become accustomed to it."

Sarah smiled. "It does feel like a holiday,
doesn't it? But do not call me Miss Hayes any
longer when we are in private, Charlotte. It
makes me feel quite ancient, and although I
sometimes feel it, I assure you I am only five and
twenty. I am no longer your teacher, after all, but
your companion, and we are old friends, are we
not?"

Charlotte's eyes widened. "Yes, I suppose we are. And I do not think you ancient, far from it. You are very beautiful. I have often wanted to tell you so."

Sarah's brows rose in surprise. "Well, now you have. Thank you."

"And it is not just that this feels like a holiday," she continued. "I am more comfortable with you than with anyone else."

"At the moment, yes," Sarah said, carefully. "But your experience of the world is very limited as yet, Charlotte. I am sure you will make many friends when you have gained the confidence that will come from being part of a family again."

"I may make friends," Charlotte agreed, "but I am not at all sure I will find a husband, or even if I want one. Discussing Great Aunt Augusta's situation has made me consider my own. I am more fortunate than she was, you see. I have some money of my own, enough to live comfortably in a small way. If I do not take, or find someone whom I wish to marry and find myself in need of a companion – a permanent companion – I would be very happy if you came to live with me. Do say you will, at least, consider it, Miss…Sarah."

Sarah knew she should nip this fantasy in the

bud, but Charlotte's eyes were shining with hope and she could not do it.

"I do not think you will have need of me, my dear," she said gently. "But if such an unlikely situation should arise, you may be certain I shall not dismiss it out of hand."

Charlotte seemed satisfied.

"Now, come, we will retire, for I think we should make an early start."

They had just reached the top of the stairs when Charlotte suddenly exclaimed, "Oh, I have left my reticule in the parlour."

"Never mind, you scatterbrain. I shall fetch it for you, just as soon as I have seen you to your door."

She found it hooked over the corner of a chair. A proud little smile touched her lips as she picked up the reticule Charlotte had fashioned from a scrap of blue velvet. It was beautifully embroidered with a circle of white roses. Her initials were neatly set inside it. She slipped the cord over her slender wrist.

"You may be scatterbrained, at times, Charlotte Fletcher," she murmured, "but when you set your mind to something, you are very accomplished."

As she stepped back into the hallway, a gentleman with brown, wavy hair, rather hard grey eyes, and a handsome countenance, strode out of the coffee room. He came to an abrupt halt when he saw her. Their eyes met. Both widened in surprise. Sarah took an involuntary step backwards as her stomach suddenly twisted into knots and her mouth went dry.

"Sarah!" he said, coming towards her.

She retreated a few more steps into the parlour, but he followed her, shut the door, and leaned back against it, his eyes slowly drinking in her appearance.

"Sarah," he said again, this time more softly.

Her chin rose and she found her voice.

"Miss Hayes to you, sir."

As if suddenly remembering his manners, he straightened and offered her a shallow bow. "Miss Hayes, then. It is good to see you. Whatever are you doing here?"

Her eyes flashed. It was good to see her? How dare he? He had certainly not felt that way the last time she had seen him.

"I do not think that is any concern of yours, Lord Turnbull," she said, pleased that despite the uncomfortable, hot feeling inside her, her voice remained cool and calm. "Now, if you will excuse me, there is someone waiting for me upstairs."

"Let them wait," he said, coming closer.

She retreated a few more steps but then felt the hard, unyielding edge of the dining table behind her. She flinched as Lord Turnbull raised his hand and cupped her cheek.

"I have dreamed about you many times over the years," he murmured. "I wonder if I am dreaming now?"

Sarah wrinkled her nose as his sickly sweet breath washed over her face. She noticed that his eyes were bloodshot.

"You are not dreaming, sir. You are drunk," she said scathingly. "Now, please, move aside so I can go about my business."

He carried on as if he had not heard her. "I did not want to let you go," he said. "But I had no choice. You were not what I thought you were."

"Then we were both disappointed in that regard. Now stand aside, sir."

When he still did not move, she raised her hands, placed them flat against his chest, and attempted to push him away. He merely laughed and placed his own over them.

"You were not always so eager to escape me. I will let you go, but I will take the kiss that I have dreamed of so often before I do."

He released one of her hands and his arm snaked around her slim waist. She leaned back as far as she could, but he bent over her and lowered his head.

"I am going to enjoy this," he murmured, closing his eyes.

Sarah's free hand scrabbled over the table. It had not yet been cleared, and her fingers curled around the handle of a large, stoneware water jug. When Lord Turnbull's lips were no more than a whisper away from her own, she twisted and swung it with all her strength in a sideways arc. It caught him on the temple and he crumpled to the ground.

She straightened and moved swiftly towards the door. "Not as much as I enjoyed that," she muttered.

She turned, surprised, when she heard a faint chuckle. Lord Turnbull pushed himself up from the floor and sat with his back against a chair.

"You vixen," he said, gingerly touching his head. "I deserved that, I suppose. You were right, of course. I have been drinking. But don't run away. I believe you have sobered me up. Tell me where you have been, and what you have been doing."

Sarah looked at the man she had once thought she loved and felt nothing but scorn. "I have nothing at all to say to you, sir."

She turned and left the room with icy composure. As soon as the door closed firmly behind her, however, all semblance of calm left her. She picked up her skirts and fled up the stairs, her heart thumping in her chest and a fiery anger throbbing through her veins. How dare he touch her! Breathe on her! Talk to her! Never mind attempt to kiss her! He was a cad, a scoundrel, a worm beneath her feet!

His estate, she knew, lay somewhere north of Sherborne, and so it was not perhaps surprising that he should occasionally pass this way. But for him to be here today, and to come into the hall at the exact same moment as herself was outrageous, preposterous, not to mention extremely unfortunate. Fate was a cruel master.

She entered her room, locked the door, and strode over to the washstand. She gave a ragged laugh and then splashed cold water over her face. She thought she had overcome the temper that the red in her hair hinted at, years ago. But apparently she was mistaken. It had merely been chained up and buried with the memories of her old life. Until today, when the lid of her Pandora's box had been wrenched open, and bitterness, anger, and betrayal had flown out.

Her head whipped round as she heard a knock on the door.

"Who is it?"

"Only me. Did you find it?"

Charlotte's gentle tones calmed her, and by the time she opened the door, all traces of her discomposure had been erased from the smooth contours of her face.

CHAPTER 2

Lord Seymore paced up and down the dimly lit landing of his aunt's townhouse in Brook Street. He did not wish to be there. He had intended to surprise Charlotte, and escort her and Miss Hayes into Dorset; he had done little enough for the child over the years, after all. But his mother's sister, Lady Cravensby, had foiled him.

He had come up to Town to purchase a new pair of matching chestnuts from Tattersalls, (horses were one of his few extravagances), and had been on the point of setting out for Bath when a note was delivered to his house in Mount Street. His aunt's latest doctor had assured him of her imminent demise. Irritation rather than concern had been his immediate reaction to this news. It was not the first time he had received such a missive and he had not taken it at all seriously.

Having failed to provide her lord with a child, Lady Cravensby had, over the years, retreated behind a series of mysterious illnesses, all of which, she was sure, would at last release her from this cruel world. It seemed that this time, however, she was to be proved correct.

Lord Seymore had no fondness for her at all, and would not mourn her passing. She had never been able to think of anyone but herself. His mother's death had been nothing more to her than an opportunity to acquire a weak heart. And when Lord Cravensby, who had enjoyed a string of high flyers, and was, perhaps understandably, never at home, had had the good sense to cock up his toes, that heart had been forever broken.

Even so, when he had suddenly found himself the guardian of his young cousin, Miss Charlotte Fletcher, he had approached his aunt for some advice and perhaps some assistance in the matter. He had thought that they might be able to help each other. Lady Cravensby would finally be able to fill the hollow void, which she had often assured him had been created by her lack of a child, and Charlotte would be provided with a home and the gentleness and care that only a female could supply.

He had been disappointed in this quest, however.

"But, Justin," she had said in a faint voice, "she is not even a blood relative of mine. She is a Fletcher. And how can I be expected to care for another when my own delicate health is always so precarious?"

"And am I not also a Fletcher, ma'am?"

She had become suddenly faint and resorted to her weapon of choice; her smelling salts. "Do not be so provoking, Justin. Send the child to school."

Feeling that it would be quite heartless to send her away so soon, he had installed her at Winbourne, his country estate, with a governess. But her silence had been unnerving and her loneliness, palpable. A friend had told him that his sister had been very happy at Miss Wolfraston's Seminary, and so he had taken her there, hoping that she might benefit from the company of other girls.

His aunt had then accused him of being devoid of all feeling. When he had, exasperated, reminded her that he had only been following her advice, she had suffered a spasm.

But that advice had proved to be sound,

after all. Once Miss Hayes had arrived, Charlotte had seemed much happier. He had, that first year, expected his ward to join him for the summer at Winbourne, but she had assured him that she would much rather remain at the seminary. When Miss Wolfraston had informed him that Miss Hayes always remained to take care of the year-round boarders, he had been reassured.

It had not occurred to him, at first, that it could be the same Miss Hayes who had captivated him when he had come down from university and for the first time, experienced the season. It was impossible to imagine such a beautiful, vital creature living such a tame existence. But Charlotte had described her to him in such glowing terms that his curiosity was aroused.

When Miss Hayes had repeatedly refused to allow him to thank her personally for her kind services to his cousin, he had begun to suspect that it might, indeed, be her. He had asked Miss Wolfraston about her background and qualifications. She had not been very forthcoming, but had assured him that she was a very accomplished young lady who had moved in the first circles until she had fallen on hard times. Then, he had been certain. He had finally accepted her wishes, understanding the awkwardness of her situation.

Lord Seymore had been summoned back to Winbourne not long after her engagement to Turnbull. His calf love was soon forgotten when he discovered that his father had suffered a stroke. Although his parent had remained perfectly lucid, he had suffered some paralysis on his left side. He had spent the next eighteen months at home running the estate and keeping his father in good spirits. He had seemed to be making a slow recovery, and so it was a cruel blow when he had suffered a second stroke, this one, fatal.

He paused and took a deep breath as a door further along the landing opened. He might not have any reason to love his aunt, but he could not let her die without any member of her family by her side.

A man with bushy sideburns and a grave demeanour stepped out and nodded. "It will not be long now, sir."

Lord Seymore came slowly towards him. "What is it she suffers from, doctor?"

"I cannot give you a precise diagnosis, I am afraid. It is some sort of wasting disease."

He nodded and went into the chamber. The curtains were shut and only a single candle burned on a table by the bed. The room was gloomy and stuffy. A stale smell permeated the thick, heavy air. A priest stood over the figure in the bed, murmuring words of comfort, assuring Lady Cravensby of her safe deliverance into the hands of the Lord. He stepped back as Lord Seymore approached.

Pity stirred in his breast as he looked down at his aunt. She seemed shrunken in the huge bed. Her face was pinched and sharp, leached of all colour apart from the dark smudges under her closed eyes. Her lips were slightly parted as she drew shallow, rasping breaths of air into her labouring lungs.

He covered her thin, dry hand with his own, ashamed now of his earlier thoughts. Every person deserved to be mourned by someone.

"Justin? Is it you?"

Her words were the faintest whisper. He leaned closer.

"I am here, Aunt."

"I should have taken that child, Charlotte."

"Do not disturb yourself. She is happy enough."

Her eyes flickered open. "I have never loved anyone, perhaps I could have loved her. But I have always been selfish. No one will remember me with kindness."

Lord Seymore saw regret and fear in her eyes.

"I will," he said gently.

"Thank you." Her eyes closed and a faint sigh escaped her. Her face relaxed as a small smile curled her thin lips.

He straightened, his jaw rigid, surprised to discover his eyes were moist.

"She is gone," he said softly.

Sarah and Charlotte arrived at Priddleton Hall at noon. The sky was overcast and a persistent drizzle obscured the view from the coach window. They only had a brief glimpse of a looming grey stone building before the butler showed them into a huge hall.

Sarah felt Charlotte step closer as her eyes swept around the vast chamber. Even though the slightly arched ceiling was very high, and the outside wall benefited from two tall, mullioned windows, the oak panelling that stretched from floor to ceiling darkened the room. No carpet softened the flagged stone floor, and the upright chairs that lined the walls had uncomfortable looking carved backs and threadbare velvet seats. A large fireplace dominated the wall at the end of the room, but although two huge logs burned there, no trace of warmth could be detected in the chill air.

Sarah turned to the butler. "The house must be quite old, I think. This room is certainly very impressive."

"The great hall was built at the end of the fifteenth century, I believe, ma'am," he said, a note of pride in his voice.

"And has all the attendant inconveniences," came a dry voice.

A lady wearing a rich, ruby coloured turban came briskly towards them, wrapping her exquisitely embroidered cashmere shawl more firmly about her. "No matter how warm it is outside this room remains as cool as an ice house."

Sarah bowed politely and Charlotte curtsied to her great aunt.

"Miss Hayes, Charlotte, welcome to Priddleton Hall. Now, let us dispense with the formalities, for I can't abide 'em! Charlotte, why you should curtsy so deeply to me, I can't imagine; I am not royalty. I was very happy as plain Mrs Fancot. You could have knocked me down with a feather when I became Lady Carstairs. I had no expectation of it; it was far more likely that Mr Fancot and I would succumb to the rigours of the Indian climate before his brother would stick his spoon in the wall, after all. But come, I don't know what I'm about letting you catch your death in this gloomy old hall."

She turned to the butler, who had stiffened, a mischievous twinkle brightening her grey eyes. "When you have overcome your indignation at my irreverent words, Riddle, perhaps you could ask Mrs Baines to bring some tea to the drawing room?"

Riddle bowed, his face impassive.

"I shouldn't tease him," Lady Carstairs said, leading them through a door that led off the hall. "But I can't resist it. He is inordinately proud of this draughty old house. Here we are. I think you will find this room far more comfortable."

Although the drawing room was also covered in dark panelling, two large, wide windows allowed more light in, the ceiling was much lower, and the floorboards were largely covered by a carpet. The fire was lit, and the room felt cosy and warm.

"I have not yet acclimatised to the conditions here in England," Lady Carstairs said. "I always have a fire lit, but if you are too hot, feel free to move your chairs a little further away from the hearth."

Once they were all comfortably seated, her sharp eyes softened as they rested on Charlotte.

"You are very like your mother, my dear."

Charlotte smiled shyly. "Thank you, Great Aunt—"

"You may drop the 'great'. Not only is it quite a mouthful, it makes me sound a hundred years old, and it is patently untrue. I am many things, Charlotte, as you will discover, but great is not one of them."

Charlotte's eyes widened, and she looked at her great aunt a little uncertainly. But although her tone of voice seemed to be naturally astringent, her eyes held a humour that took the sting from her words. She smiled tentatively.

"That is better," approved Lady Carstairs. "You may be sure that if I am ever displeased with you, Charlotte, you will be left in no doubt of it. But I have not invited you here to bully you. I detest bullies. Lord Seymore told me you were a shy little butterfly, and I see that it is true. But we shall spread your delicate wings, my child, and watch you fly."

"I will do my best, Aunt."

"Then I can ask no more. We can none of us change our natures, after all, but we can learn to control and refine them."

She paused as the tea tray was brought in.

After handing them both a cup, her gaze turned to Sarah. "Miss Hayes, you have a look of old Berty Beaumont about you. Your grandfather was a friend of Lady Brabacombe, to whom I used to be a companion. Only man I ever knew who could put her in her place. He brought you there once when you were barely higher than my knee, you cannot have been much more than four. I have never forgotten it."

"I am afraid I do not remember it at all," Sarah admitted.

A wicked grin curled Lady Carstairs' lips. "Then I shall remind you. Your grandfather had a very quick temper." Her eyes rested on Sarah's hair for a moment. "I expect you have one too, although I am sure you have learned to control it."

Charlotte suddenly sat very upright. "It is not true," she declared, quite vehemently. "I will not have a word said against Miss Hayes."

"That's my gal," approved Lady Carstairs, but she quirked an enquiring brow at her relative's companion.

Sarah suddenly laughed. "It is quite true. I have been known to fly into the boughs when provoked, but as you say, I have learned to master the impulse."

Hitting Lord Turnbull over the head with a

jug did not count, it had been an aberration, and she had only been defending herself, after all.

"We shall see," said Lady Carstairs. "I don't expect a handful of schoolgirls really put it to the test. Besides, I think many a fool would be better for a sharp set-down. Now, where was I?"

"Although I am not at all sure that it is in my interests to remind you, ma'am, you were with Lady Brabacombe, I believe."

"Oh yes. Well, your grandfather and Lady Brabacombe were arguing about something or other, it might have been Pitt's Treasonable Practices Act, I am not sure; they were always arguing about politics. Things got rather heated; again not unusual, and she called your grandfather a perfidious radical with more hair than wit. She did not mean it, of course, but you took exception to her tone."

"It could not have been her words," Sarah said wryly, "for I could not have understood them."

"That will become clear," agreed Lady Carstairs. "You marched over to her, put your little hands on your hips, and informed her in no uncertain terms that she was a very rude, old lady, and that there was nothing wrong with your grandpapa's hair. You then turned on your heel, marched back to him, and informed him that you would not stay in the rude lady's house one moment longer."

Sarah groaned. "What a precocious child I was."

Lady Carstairs chuckled. "I wouldn't lose any sleep over it, if I were you. Your grandfather went into paroxysms of laughter, and Lady Brabacombe soon joined in. You had only stated the truth, after all. She was quite aware of the fact that she was a rude, old lady. She took some pride in it."

"As do you, I think, ma'am."

Charlotte gasped, but Lady Carstairs gave a shout of laughter. "You are right, of course. I have never been able to abide all the mealy-mouthed platitudes that govern polite society."

The door opened on her words and two gentlemen entered the room. The elder of the two was tall and thin. Although he had more than sixty years in his dish, there was a sprightliness about him. Beneath a shock of thick, white hair, a pair of faded blue eyes glimmered with amusement. The deep creases that edged them suggested he was not a stranger to laughter.

"What would you know of polite society, my dear? You avoid it whenever possible. Or at least you did until you came here."

"Hrmf! You talk as if I had a choice. Our neighbours will insist on calling however much I discourage 'em! Wherever have you been hiding Carstairs? If Riddle did not inform you immediately of our guests' arrival, I will own myself amazed."

"As I would not wish you to suffer such a tiresome emotion, my dear, you may rest assured that our assiduous butler did indeed perform that office with his usual promptitude. I thought only to give you all a moment alone."

He turned to his guests, a twinkle in his eyes, and bowed. "Miss Hayes, Miss Fletcher, I am delighted to make your acquaintance."

Once they had replied in kind, he stepped forwards and took Charlotte's hands. "We have never been a prolific family, so I must tell you, my dear, that it fills me with pleasure to have acquired another relative. I hope you will be very happy here and would be very pleased if you would refer to me as Uncle Oliver."

Charlotte coloured and said all that was polite.

He turned to the man who still hovered by the door, his eyes fixed on Charlotte. "Come, Charles, there is no need for you to hang back, you are not only my steward, you are also family, after all."

The gentleman dutifully came forwards. He was rather stocky and of a moderate height. His only distinguishing features were a pair of intense, dark brown eyes and a slightly hooked nose. The latter attribute gave the clue to his ancestry. A long line of Fancots, including Lord Carstairs, shared it.

"Let me introduce you to Mr Fancot. He is the son of a distant cousin of mine. It is thanks to his unflagging vigilance and care that we have come home to a thriving estate."

Mr Fancot seemed embarrassed by this fulsome praise. He bowed and offered them a small smile. "I could do no less when the late earl sponsored my education and brought me here once it was completed. But I have done no more than any self-respecting steward would have done, I am sure."

"Although your modesty is laudable, Charles, I must disagree. By the time we had wrapped up our affairs in India to our satisfaction and made the journey home, it had been two years since my brother had passed. Yet everything here was in such good order, no one would have suspected that Priddleton had been without a master for so long. I expect Filton is also in just as good order."

Mr Fancot coloured. "You are too kind. As

for Filton, I received a letter from Mr Danesby, who is our tenant there, a few days ago. He is moving back to Derbyshire to support his widowed sister sometime next week. He has a five-year lease on the property that is about to expire. It has all happened so quickly that I have had no time to inform you or discuss what you would like to do with the property. I had fully expected him to renew it and so I have been taken a little by surprise. I will need to spend a few days there to see what needs to be done. Perhaps you would like to come with me, sir?"

"Perhaps I will, Charles. It is only half a day's ride, after all."

A very neat lady dressed in black came into the room.

"I've prepared a nuncheon for our guests, my lady. I thought perhaps they might like me to show them to their rooms so they can freshen up first."

Lady Carstairs sighed. "Of course, Mrs Baines. I would have sent for you in a moment or two. It never ceases to surprise me that, although we have far fewer servants here, everything is run so much more efficiently than it was in India."

Her tone was rather wistful, and her husband smiled indulgently down at her.

"And if my memory serves me correctly, my dear, you were always complaining that you could not move for tripping over a servant, but whatever order you gave seemed to take at least half an hour to be put into execution. Yet you would not get rid of any of them."

"Of course, I would not, Carstairs. They depended on us. It was just their way. Besides, everything always got done in the end."

Lord Carstairs grinned at Mr Fancot. "It was one of the reasons we were so long in returning, Charles. We had many people interested in purchasing our garden house in Calcutta, but Lady Carstairs insisted on vetting them all. She wished to be sure that they would keep all of our servants and treat them in a way she approved of."

"Do not get me started on the disgraceful way so many of our countrymen and women treated the native inhabitants of the country, Carstairs, or Mrs Baines' nuncheon will grow stale on the table!"

Sarah and Charlotte followed the housekeeper from the room.

"I have prepared rooms for you both in the newer west wing," she informed them. "It was added towards the end of the seventeenth century, and the rooms are larger and brighter there."

"Thank you, Mrs Baines," Charlotte said politely.

The housekeeper's rather stern countenance, softened.

"And I have assigned each of you a personal maid as you have not brought your own. I have trained them up myself seeing as Lady Carstairs has brought her own maid back from India. I am sure I have nothing to say against her, keeps herself to herself mostly and seems a very pleasant sort, but she can hardly be expected to know how we do things here. We may not have as many staff at Priddleton as Lady Carstairs is used to, but we have enough."

CHAPTER 3

B y the time Lord Seymore had attended his aunt's funeral and listened to the reading of her will, almost a week had passed. He could not regret the delay, however, for only he and the current Lord Cravensby had been present. That gentleman had been as surprised as Lord Seymore that one of the dowager's many illnesses had finally carried her off.

That he had displayed no false grief over the demise of his uncle's wife was to his credit, and Lord Seymore was grateful that he had not been guilty of such a show of hypocrisy. Unfortunately, neither had he shown the gravity that Lord Seymore felt the occasion deserved. Lord Cravensby's happiness at finally gaining possession of the town house his uncle had left to the use of his widow whilst she lived, had appeared to govern his every action and thought. He had dragged Lord Seymore through all the main rooms, describing in tedious detail the changes he and his good lady would make to the establishment. The only dent in this unseemly show of enthusiasm occurred when he discovered he was not to benefit further by any gift in Lady Cravensby's will.

It was with some relief that Lord Seymore left behind the hot, dusty, and rather malodorous streets of the metropolis. Two days of country air restored his usual calm good humour, however.

As he came to the neat, wide streets of Priddleton village, he slowed his curricle the better to observe the charming thatched cottages that lined the way. When he came to the square, his eyes dwelled for a moment on the rather fine castellated church tower. A grin twitched his lips as he observed a grimacing gargoyle glaring down at him. For some reason Lady Carstairs came to mind.

As he had not yet had the pleasure of making her acquaintance in person, he could not but feel that this comparison was unworthy of him. But her letters had held barely a modicum of politeness; indeed, they had been both severe and condemnatory in style. They had, however, left him in no doubt that she had Charlotte's best interests at heart. Even so, the nagging worry that such an outspoken and redoubtable lady might frighten her half out of her wits, had plagued him all week. Only the knowledge that Miss Hayes would stand a friend to her in his absence, had enabled him to bear the disruption to his plans with any degree of equanimity. He had not dawdled on the journey however, and had arrived a day earlier than planned.

The parsonage lay fifty yards to the east of the church. It was a fine three-storey building with a walled garden behind. Like all the other properties in the village, it was well maintained. The Carstairs appeared to be conscientious and generous landlords.

Lord Seymore brought his curricle to a halt, amused, as he saw a gentleman creep around the corner of the building. This person glanced furtively in the direction of the church before scurrying down the path from the parsonage. Whilst his high shirt points, pale pink pantaloons, and blue coat of bath superfine, would not have seemed at all out of the way if he had been strolling down St James, or walking along

Bond Street, in this rustic village he stuck out like a sore thumb.

As this gentleman's attention remained fixed on the church, he did not immediately perceive the curricle that was drawn up on the other side of the road.

"Good day, Bamber," Lord Seymore said, as he stepped through the gate.

The gentleman gave a start. His wide eyes, blond locks, and amiable countenance gave him the appearance of a startled cherub.

"Seymore," he spluttered. "What on earth are you doing in this backwater?"

"Is there any reason I should not be here?" he said, smiling.

"None at all, old fellow. Delighted to see you. The more of us the better. Do tell me you are staying somewhere close by," he said, a little desperately.

Used to Sir Horace Bamber's eccentric ways, Lord Seymore was not at all surprised by his somewhat disjointed remarks.

"I am," he confirmed. "I will be putting up at Priddleton Hall."

"Capital. It's only a stone's throw from here. I say, old chap, I was just about to pop down to The Plough for a quick tipple. Care to join me?"

Sir Horace glanced over his shoulder as he

proffered the invitation. Lord Seymore followed his gaze and saw a tall, rather thin gentleman, dressed in a black suit and neat white cravat, coming down the path from the church.

"Perhaps another time—"

He broke off as Sir Horace hurried around the curricle and climbed up next to him.

"Priddleton Hall did you say? I'll come with you, Seymore. Ought to pay my respects to Lord Carstairs after all. He's bound to have a fine claret, don't you think?"

Lord Seymore obligingly flicked his whip and the curricle moved off.

"Having not visited him before, I really could not say. However, I wouldn't be at all surprised if you are right. Whatever wine he has in his cellar must be vastly superior to anything you are likely to find at the local inn, at all events."

"You're right, by Jove. A good thing you came by when you did, Seymore. But you still haven't told me why you did come by. If you don't know him, why are you paying Lord Carstairs a visit?"

"His wife is the great aunt of my ward, Miss Charlotte Fletcher. She is, at present, a guest in their house."

Sir Horace's brow creased in thought. "That name rings a bell but I can't quite place her.

Probably one of the many young ladies my mother introduced me to last season. Can't remember the half of them. It becomes a dashed awkward business when I bump into them again, I can tell you."

Lord Seymore chuckled. "You need not worry in this instance, Bamber. There is not the least likelihood that you have met Miss Fletcher for she is not out, and has until very recently been at Miss Wolfraston's Seminary for Young Ladies."

Sir Horace's eyes widened. "You don't say. Then I have heard her name. I became acquainted with two other young ladies from that very same seminary not so long ago, in Cheltenham. Very fine gals they were too. They mentioned that they had a friend called Charlotte. Seemed very fond of her."

"I am glad to hear it. I think you must be referring to Miss Montagu and Lady Georgianna Voss, as those two names were most often on her lips."

"That's it," Sir Horace said, beaming. "If she's anything like them, I will be delighted to meet her. They weren't at all like the other young ladies of my acquaintance."

Lord Seymore raised a dark brow. It was well known that Sir Horace turned into a gibbering wreck in the company of young ladies. "In what way did they differ from those other ladies?"

"No simpering nonsense for a start. I found them very frank and friendly. Knew exactly where you were with them. Weren't on the catch for a husband, either. It was very refreshing, I assure you."

"It must have been," Lord Seymore murmured.

He did not speak from first-hand experience, as he did not go up to Town all that often; he much preferred the country. When he did visit, it was usually on a matter of business, or to pay a visit to his tailor. On those occasions he usually met up with other friends who were not overly fond of the whirl of social gaieties on offer. Sir Horace was one of them, when his mama wasn't insisting that he accompany her somewhere or other, usually much against his will.

The thought that he should begin thinking about settling down had been floating about in the back of Lord Seymore's mind for some time, but in a vague, nebulous sort of way. The death of his aunt had brought it more sharply into focus, however. He was very fond of Winbourne, his estate near Lymington in Hampshire, and would not like to see it fall into the hands of some obscure relative who might prove as grasping as Lord Cravensby. Perhaps it was time he set up his stable.

He would not look for his bride in Town, however. He did not intend to change his habits. He had nothing against a rational amount of amusement; it was not unknown for him to attend a concert or the theatre, but he would not wish to saddle himself with a lady who would easily grow bored of country living and be forever plaguing him to take her to London for the season. He would look for a respectable, gentle girl, who lived locally and would be happy with a visit to the assembly rooms in Lymington. Off the top of his head, he could think of at least two candidates who might fit this description. And one of them, he considered a friend. Friendship was as good a basis for marriage as anything else, surely.

As they turned through the gates of Priddleton Hall, it occurred to Lord Seymore that although Sir Horace often tried to evade the balls that littered the social calendar in London, he could think of no reason for his furtive behaviour in a rural village. Unless he had been ruffling the feathers of the local maidens, but as Sir Horace was not in the petticoat line, this was highly unlikely.

"I do not wish to be overly inquisitive, Bamber, but is there any particular reason you are avoiding the vicar? His appearance does not seem to be unduly alarming."

Sir Horace looked a little sheepish. "He's my brother, Loftus. Thought I'd pay him a visit. I'm trying to escape the latest distant relative my mother has invited to catch my interest."

Lord Seymore glanced down at his friend, a satirical gleam in his eye.

"But now, it seems, you are escaping your brother."

The sheepish look was replaced with one of outraged indignation. "I should think I am. Only arrived yesterday, and he's already drawn up a list of activities he feels will be good for my soul! Says I'm too concerned with worldly things and ought to become better acquainted with the lot of the common man, so I will develop a better understanding of those it is my duty to protect!"

Lord Seymore's shoulders began to shake. "Dare I ask what tasks this list contains?"

"Give your imagination free rein, Seymore," Sir Horace said, waving his hand in an expansive gesture. "On the other hand, don't, for I doubt you, or anyone else who isn't queer in their attic, could think his demands reasonable. The list is extremely comprehensive. Everything from chopping wood, feeding his chickens, picking his peas, to teaching his servants to read, and visiting the poor."

Lord Seymore tried to envisage his friend attempting any of these tasks and failed dismally. But he did Sir Horace an injustice to overlook the last item, as he soon discovered.

"I told him I'd visited the workhouse in Cheltenham, not to mention having a considerable amount of food that was left over from an al fresco nuncheon I had catered for, delivered there. And what do you think he said?"

Sir Horace's face was quite flushed and his sense of ill-usage patently apparent.

"I cannot imagine, dear fellow. Enlighten me."

"He said that giving them the crumbs from my table was a start, but that I was a fribble, a fop, more interested in my wardrobe than the plight of my fellow man!"

Lord Seymore's brows rose in surprise. "That seems a little harsh."

"Harsh! Harsh!" spluttered Sir Horace, who had by now worked himself into quite a taking. "It was beyond harsh. It was uncalled for, unfair, and downright unjust."

"Forgive me for asking," Lord Seymore said

softly, "but have you, er, ticked any of these items off your list?"

"No, I have not had the chance even if I wished to, which I don't. I got halfway down it and thought I'd soften the shock with a drink in The Plough. Loftus makes his own mead wine from honey. I have been assured it is an acquired taste, but I have not yet acquired it."

"Poor fellow. Tell me, if your brother is so demanding and unreasonable, what made you visit him? Surely facing whatever female your mother had lined up would have been the easier option?"

Sir Horace sighed and shook his head, bewilderment writ clear in his moss green eyes.

"I don't pretend to understand it. You know I have a wretched memory, Seymore, but it not so wretched that I would forget how my own brother behaves. He is usually a jolly good sort. He likes to tease me now and then, but in a gentle way."

"Perhaps that is it, then," Lord Seymore suggested. "He is having a joke at your expense."

Sir Horace considered this for a moment and then a look of relief swept over his face. "Of course! That must be it! There can be no other explanation. Unless that mead wine has curdled his insides and put him out of temper, which wouldn't surprise me, for it is as potent as it is unpalatable."

"Oh ho! You did try a fair amount of it then?"

His irony was completely lost on Sir Horace.

"Would have been rude not to."

Lady Carstairs did not receive visitors on a Friday and so Riddle was not expecting any. He had informed the new footman that he needed to check the stocks in the wine cellar and did not wish to be disturbed. Even though he had only recently been taken on, the footman knew this meant that he was having a nap and would tear a strip off him if he were disturbed.

He was aware that they were expecting a visitor the following day, and was not too flustered by the arrival of Lord Seymore, who he knew to be the guardian of Miss Fletcher, but his eyes widened as he saw Sir Horace. He gulped. He was loath to discommode the very fine looking gentleman, but he was even more afraid to disturb Lady Carstairs on a Friday with an uninvited guest.

By the time he had gathered his wits, however, both gentlemen had stepped past him into the hall and were offering him their hats. The opportunity to deny him entry had passed.

"Lady Carstairs is expecting me, I believe,"

Lord Seymore said gently, as the footman continued to stand strangely transfixed before him.

A resigned look crossed the young man's face. He laid the hats on a convenient table and bowed.

"Of course, sir. Come this way."

He led them up the stairs and along a gallery hung with paintings of the Carstair ancestors. Whether the many eyes that followed them looked down with expressions of benevolence or hauteur was difficult to tell, for the dark wainscoting that prevailed in the older part of the house, seemed to absorb what little light there was.

The footman paused for a moment in front of a large, iron-studded door and took a deep breath. He opened it and announced the guests, only the slight break in his voice spoiling the impassive delivery he had strived for.

Lord Seymore and Sir Horace stepped into the room, their smiles freezing on their lips at the unexpected tableau before them. Swathes of light drapes covered the dark walls. A foreign, exotic scene had been painstakingly embroidered onto them. A long winding river flowed from one to the other. It was dotted with vessels, from long narrow rowing boats with upturned ends, to three-masted ships. Colourful butterflies rested on unfamiliar blooms, or hovered in the air, elephants roamed through the arches of banyan trees, and tigers stalked through long strands of grass.

Just as exotic was the slender, dusky skinned lady, clothed in a long flowing red robe, which fell to ankles that were encircled by small bells. She dipped and swayed gracefully to the music of a short-necked string instrument. The nearest thing to it either gentleman had seen was a violin, but the body was boxlike, and it was held vertically in front of the player who drew a bow back and forth across its strings.

That player was Lady Carstairs. She also wore a long flowing robe of red muslin, decorated with gold thread around the hem. Upon her head was a green turban. Her eyes were closed as she teased a low, haunting melody from the instrument.

It took a moment for both dancer and player to register the intrusion, so lost were they in their performance. But Charlotte jumped to her feet and came forwards with her hands outstretched.

"Justin. We did not expect you until tomorrow."

His lips relaxed into a more natural smile as he looked down into the face of his ward. He felt gratified to see genuine pleasure at his arrival shining in her eyes. It was immediately apparent to him that his fears had been unwarranted. One swift glance about the room had informed him that Miss Hayes was not present, yet Charlotte showed no signs of trepidation at being left alone with her aunt, or any awkwardness at being discovered in so unusual a situation.

"Brinoo, who is Lady Carstairs' maid, has been showing me some of the dances of her own country. I have never witnessed anything so graceful or beautiful."

Lord Seymore glanced up at the maid, but she averted her face and rushed from the room. Lady Carstairs got to her feet, a frown between her eyes, and he bowed respectfully to her.

"I am sorry to have brought your performance to an early close, ma'am," he said. "You seem very proficient on that instrument. I do not believe I have ever heard anything quite like it."

"It is a sarangi," she said, looking at him closely. "You do not object, then, to me exposing your ward to the Indian culture?"

Lord Seymore looked surprised. "Why should you not share some of your knowledge with her? I admittedly only saw a very little of the dance, but I saw nothing objectionable in it."

"That is because there was nothing to take objection to, Lord Seymore, if you have an open mind. It seems you do. I am pleased. You are not the fool I expected you to be."

His amused glance swept over her unusual, yet very feminine dress, and came to rest on her face. She held herself very upright, and raised her chin in response to his close scrutiny. Her silvery grey eyes held a hint of challenge. He thought her very handsome. She certainly bore no resemblance to the gargoyle on the church tower.

"And you, ma'am, are not quite what I expected either. I am sorry that I seem to have embarrassed your maid."

"That cannot now be helped, but it is unfortunate. This room is for my private use. I do not receive visitors here. Brinoo is very modest. She would never have agreed to perform if she had thought there would be any danger of us being interrupted. I cannot think how it comes about that you were brought up. I have made my wishes very clear on this matter."

"Ah, that explains why your footman looked so confounded at our arrival."

Lady Carstairs glanced at the open door, but the young man had made good his escape.

"Ha! He's made a run for it. But it is Riddle, my butler, who will have some explaining to do," she said with some relish.

Lord Seymore was aware of a feeling of sympathy for Riddle.

"May I introduce my friend, Sir Horace Bamber, ma'am?"

Lady Carstairs' gaze swivelled in his direction, dwelling for a moment on his fine apparel. "Bamber? Are you related to our worthy vicar?"

"Brother, ma'am. I'm paying him a visit. Thought I'd come and pay my respects. Didn't mean to intrude."

"No, I'm sure you did not. But the fact remains that you have intruded and no doubt have formed a very odd opinion of me."

Sir Horace looked surprised. "Haven't formed any opinion at all, ma'am. Wouldn't dream of it. Not my place to. But now I think of it, that dress is very becoming. Unusual, but dashed eye-catching. I expect it is all the rage in India."

Seeing the satirical gleam that lit Lady Carstairs' fine eyes, and feeling fairly certain that she was about to wither his friend with a scathing comment, Lord Seymore intervened.

"Charlotte, Sir Horace has recently made the acquaintance of your friends, Miss Montagu and Lady Georgianna, in Cheltenham."

Charlotte smiled shyly at him. "But that is

wonderful. Please, sit with me and tell me how they go on."

Lady Carstairs looked at Lord Seymore with reluctant approval and gave a low laugh. "Saving the lamb from the slaughter?"

Lord Seymore grinned disarmingly at her. "He has already borne much this day, ma'am."

He proceeded to recount the entertainments in store for his friend. Lady Carstairs gave a shout of laughter.

"I would give much to be able to witness him carrying out any of these tasks. If he wasn't such a fool, I would feel sorry for him."

Lord Seymore glanced quickly in his friend's direction, but he and Charlotte were in close conversation and they did not seem to have heard Lady Carstairs' remark.

"You appear to think the world is littered with fools, ma'am. Sir Horace's understanding may be no more than moderate, but I would not call him a fool. And I do feel sorry for him. Sir Horace Bamber is one of the kindest men of my acquaintance. There is nothing he would not do for a friend."

Lady Carstairs' lips twitched. "Not afraid to stand up to me, eh? Good. I can't abide toadeaters. I shall have to take your word for it, I suppose. I am very pleased with Miss Hayes by the way. Your judgement there was spot on. She is very good company for both Charlotte and myself."

"I am glad to hear it, ma'am. Did she not wish to enjoy this afternoon of Indian culture?"

"Not as much as she wished to go riding. And who can blame her? Being confined in that seminary for so long must have been torture to one who is so naturally spirited."

CHAPTER 4

Sarah was sure she would have thoroughly enjoyed the entertainment planned by Lady Carstairs, but she wished to promote the bond of affection that was rapidly growing between Charlotte and her aunt. She had become quite adept at finding excuses to leave them alone for a short while. She was sure Lady Carstairs was well aware of her motivation, for when she suddenly discovered that she had mislaid some small item, or had a slight headache and must lie down for a while, she gave her a very knowing look.

Today, she had not had to fabricate an excuse, however. When Lord Carstairs had found her wandering about his stables, enthusiastically discussing the finer points of the many fine mounts there with his head groom, Greeves, he had insisted she must feel free to make use of them, if she so desired.

"You seem to know your way around horses," he had said, smiling. "And so you will know they need exercising. You will be doing me a service, Miss Hayes, if you take them for an airing now and then."

Lady Carstairs had not objected. "Of course you must go. You have been cooped up long enough. Every Friday is my India day, so there will be many more opportunities for you to learn something about the country and its people."

She chose a spirited black mare.

"She's a bit frisky, ma'am," Greeves warned her as he bent and cupped his hands for her booted foot. "She needs a good run."

"As do I," Sarah said, springing into the saddle.

As she settled her leg over the pommel and arranged the skirts of her habit, the restless horse danced sideways across the cobbles, tossing her head.

"Patience," she said gently, holding the reins lightly but firmly, whilst exerting gentle pressure with her left leg.

"You'll do," Greeves said approvingly. "Are

you sure you don't want me to accompany you, ma'am?"

Sarah smiled confidently at the man. "No, but thank you. I shall not leave the grounds."

The house sat in many acres of rolling countryside, and once she and the mare had become accustomed to each other, she gave her her head. A wide smile curved her generous lips as they flew together over the grass. How she had missed this feeling of freedom! The simple joy of feeling the breeze on her face as the ground sped by beneath her.

For a moment, she thought she heard the thud of another set of hooves pounding the turf. She turned her head and her smile faded. There was no one there, only the ghost of a memory. How often had she turned just so, and met the gleaming eyes of her father? Many, many times. She sighed and let the memory go, it could do her no good. She blinked rapidly and gave a soft chuckle. Her father would certainly not have approved of the sudden sheen of tears that brightened her eyes.

She slowed as she approached a bridge that spanned a wide river. Dismounting, she led the horse down to a small shingle beach and let it drink. She watched the fast flowing water for a moment and then sat on the grassy bank and let her thoughts meander.

Although the duty of care she felt for Charlotte had brought her here, she was not at all sure it had been a wise decision. Lady Carstairs insisted on treating her as a valued guest rather than a mere teacher or companion. When she had come down to dinner that first night, in a sober, dark, high-necked gown, she had pulled her aside and taken her to task.

"Your grandfather would turn in his grave if he could see you. You are the daughter of a baron whatever misfortune may have befallen you. Whilst you are in my house, you will dress that part. It oppresses my spirits to see you decked out in so dismal a manner."

Sarah did not like to be told what to do. Even Miss Wolfraston allowed her a great deal of leeway, and it was not unknown for her employer to defer to her on some matters. Being a shrewd lady, she recognised that Miss Hayes had a far better understanding of the quality than she had, and she certainly did not wish to alienate her most accomplished teacher.

Sarah had stood her ground and informed Lady Carstairs coolly that she could not comply with this request, even if she wished to, as all her old gowns were gathering mothballs in the trunks that she stored in Miss Wolfraston's attic.

"I see," Lady Carstairs had said thoughtfully. "Well, I suppose I will just have to become accustomed, then."

Four days later, her trunks had arrived. She had walked into her bedchamber to discover Frampton, the maid who had been assigned to her, gleefully unpacking them.

"I've never seen so many beautiful gowns, ma'am. A few of them need furbishing up a bit, but nothing that a bit of lace or a ribbon or two won't fix."

Her maid had been quite dumbfounded when the usually mild mannered Miss Hayes had turned on her heel and stalked from the room. She had run Lady Carstairs to ground in the Egyptian garden; so named because it boasted a series of tall hedges sculpted to resemble pyramids. She had been carefully clipping a few stray shoots that detracted from their neat appearance.

"I do so enjoy gardening," she had said mildly.

"I suppose, ma'am, that is because you like to control everything and everyone about you."

Lady Carstairs had eyed her heightened colour and put down her clippers. "Not so, Miss

Hayes. I have many faults, I am sure, but that is not one of them. We both know what it is to be at another's beck and call, and I am sure it suited you as little as it did me. But I do admire beauty in its many forms. You are very beautiful, as I'm sure you know. I like to see lamb dressed as mutton as little as I like to see mutton dressed as lamb."

Sarah had seen both sympathy and understanding in Lady Carstairs' eyes and her anger had melted away.

"I am sorry, ma'am. I should not have spoken to you so."

Lady Carstairs had smiled. "Temper will out, eh? I dare say you think I have taken a great liberty in sending for your things."

"Well yes, ma'am. I do," she had said in milder tones. "But it is not that. You must understand, that part of my life is over. I have accepted that. I have striven very hard to do so and embrace the role that is now mine. I would feel almost like an imposter to put on the trappings of my old life."

"That is nonsense," Lady Carstairs had said with some asperity. "The young woman who I saw standing before me with fire in her eyes is the real Sarah Hayes. Miss Hayes of Miss Wolfraston's Seminary for Young Ladies is the imposter. You cannot deny your nature, child. You have damped down your spirit, but it is still there, a glowing ember just waiting to ignite. If you find yourself in a dark place you light a lamp, not damp it down. You have been dealt a bad hand of cards, my dear, but the way you play them is up to you."

Sarah had laughed rather wildly. "What do you suggest I do? Put on all my finery and catch myself a husband? Marry a man merely for the sake of an establishment and live with him without affection?"

"Might I point out, Miss Hayes, that it is not beyond of the realms of possibility that you might meet a man for whom you could feel some affection? But there is no chance of it if you hide yourself away. For that is exactly what you have been doing. You have a great deal of pride, some of it false."

Sarah had gasped.

"Thought that would take the wind out of your sails. There is no reason for you to put yourself beyond the reach of your own kind that I can see. I am sure you could find many pleasant situations if you tried. It is not only cur-mudgeonly old ladies who need a companion."

"Then why did you stay with one for so long, ma'am?"

She had thought that she had finally wrong-footed her opponent in this verbal battle. But Lady Carstairs had not turned a hair.

"I have never been beautiful," she had said, a little regretfully. "And there was very little chance of me finding a husband whomever I attached myself to. At least, not one I could have stomached. Besides, I grew to be quite fond of Lady Brabacombe. She amused me. But when I was given a chance, I took it."

"Yes, and you found Mr Fancot," she had said, gently.

"Indeed, I did. And if I could find a husband for whom I felt, and still feel, a great deal of affection, then so can you!"

Lord Turnbull had come into her mind, causing her to frown.

"Oh, I know you've had your wings singed once before. Made it my business to find out. And before you get on your high ropes again, my enquiries were very discreet. Had to know who was in charge of Charlotte, after all."

Sarah had stared at her resourceful hostess for a moment and then started to laugh. "You are an outrageous, interfering, old woman," she had gasped.

Lady Carstairs had taken it as a compliment and smiled broadly. "I fully admit it. But less of the old, I'm not in my dotage yet, young lady."

When she regained her composure, Sarah had smiled and said, "I am too exhausted to argue with you further. But if you think I am going to put on all my finery, you are mistaken."

Lady Carstairs had given her a very smug smile. "You will have to, my dear."

"Oh? Why is that?"

"Because, Miss Hayes, I have taken a greater liberty than you know. I have removed all your dowdy dresses and stowed them safely away."

Sarah laughed as she recalled that clincher. Fortunately, her sense of the ridiculous had overcome her indignation. They had become firm friends after that encounter.

After a period of quiet reflection, she had to admit that there had been some truth in Lady Carstairs' assertions. She had not had the maturity to accept her fall from grace with humility. Her star had shone so brightly for a short while, and she had thought it would be less painful for it to be completely extinguished rather than let it slowly fade.

But however acute Lady Carstairs' observations had been, she fully expected to return to Miss Wolfraston's seminary after this interlude. But it would not be an easy transition. As soon as the soft silk of one of her evening gowns had slid over her skin, she had felt like her old self. But she would have to pack that self away again, along with her gowns, when she returned.

She sighed. That was not for some time yet. She would deal with it when the time came. For now, she would enjoy this temporary emancipation from her humdrum existence. It was not as if she had much choice; Lady Carstairs was a force beyond her control!

The nudge of a muzzle recalled her from her reverie. She gently tickled the horse behind its ears.

"You are quite right," she murmured. "It is high time we were getting back."

"Good afternoon, Miss Hayes."

She glanced up quickly and saw Mr Fancot standing on the edge of the gently sloping bank.

"Good afternoon, sir," she said, rising swiftly to her feet. "You startled me. I was woolgathering."

He smiled. "So I gathered when you did not respond to my first greeting. I thought you might need some help getting back in your saddle."

"How thoughtful of you," she said, leading her horse back up the bank.

He tossed her up with ease. "There is a nice

ride back to the house through the woods. Would you like me to show you the way?"

"Thank you, yes. I think I have been in the sun long enough."

She followed him over the bridge and into the trees that marked thc edge of the wood. A few yards in, there was a path wide enough for them to ride side by side. The trees arched over them, casting a delightfully cool dappled shade over the rough track.

"You have a way with horses, Miss Hayes. Nyx is not always so well behaved for a stranger. More than one stable hand has been thrown when exercising her."

"Nyx?" Her brow furrowed for a moment. "Ah, I have it. Goddess of the night."

Mr Fancot's brows shot up. "Well done, ma'am. She is not one of the better known deities. I would not have thought you would teach such things at your seminary."

"I don't," Sarah said dryly. "More's the pity. But my father took a hand in my education. He thought a woman should be able to have a rational conversation on a wide variety of topics."

A rustle in the undergrowth made Nyx sidle. Mr Fancot went to grab her bridle but Sarah sent him a rather fierce glance. "Don't," she said shortly. "I am in no difficulty as you can see."

"Forgive me, ma'am," he said, rather stiffly.

"There is nothing to forgive," she said, more gently. "My father insisted I learn to handle a variety of mounts from his stable, whatever their temper. He used to say that if I could not, I deserved to be thrown."

Mr Fancot looked quite shocked at this revelation. "And were you thrown?"

Sarah laughed. "Of course. But I learned quickly so it became a very rare occurrence."

As they began to move off, another rustle issued from the bush. A deer leapt out and bounded down a smaller track. Sarah's eyes followed it and she saw a break in the trees. She glimpsed a thatched roof and a window. She thought she saw a dark figure behind its many small panes.

"Who lives there?"

"My mother and I do, ma'am. It is the dower house. I had rooms in the east wing of the hall, but when my father died last year, I brought my mother here and moved into the house with her."

"I quite understand, it must be far more comfortable than rattling around Priddleton all by yourself."

How often over the last few years had she yearned for her own home? She had often thought she would be quite satisfied with a snug little cottage in a woody glade. Her lips twitched. She had been fooling herself, of course. She would have been dreadfully bored.

Mr Fancot turned the subject.

"Does Miss Fletcher ride? We have a docile mare in the stables that would be quite suitable for a young lady."

"No," Sarah said. "It is very kind of you to think of her, but I am not at all sure she would enjoy it. She is a little timid, and I think she would baulk at the idea of climbing onto such a large creature."

"Of course. She has such a gentle nature that I should have guessed."

As they trotted into the yard, Lord Carstairs, Lord Seymore, and another gentleman she did not recognise strolled out of the stables.

Sarah felt her cheeks grow warm. She had braced herself for this encounter, but she had not expected to have to face it today. Lord Seymore strode towards her as if he would help her down. She took the reins in her right hand, removed her foot from the stirrup, moved her right leg over the pommel, and swivelled so she sat sideways. But before he could reach her she jumped, turning neatly in the air as she did so. She landed nimbly and patted Nyx.

JENNY HAMBLY

"Bravo," Lord Carstairs said. "I have never seen a woman dismount in such a fashion, but you did it very well, Miss Hayes."

"Didn't she just?" Sir Horace exclaimed. "Never seen anything like it. Marvellous, that's what it is."

Mr Fancot still sat astride his horse. He smiled down at her. "Another thing your father taught you?"

"No, I taught myself. I do not believe in depending on others for help with every little thing."

As she turned, her eyes collided with those of Lord Seymore. It had been seven years since she had seen him and although she had recognised him at a glance, she now saw that time had changed him. She thought it extremely unfair that nature often made men more distinguished and handsome as they aged, whilst it stole the youthful bloom from women.

His blue eyes were darker than she remembered, and edged by fine lines. His jaw was squarer, and his chin housed a dimple that she did not recall.

"I believe you already know Lord Seymore, Miss Hayes?" Lord Carstairs said.

Sarah nodded. "How do you do, sir?"

Lord Seymore bowed. His smile was also much more charming than she remembered.

"I am very well, Miss Hayes. I hope you will not think me rude if I do not enquire how you do? I can see that you are in the best of good health."

She was not at all sure she agreed with him, for her pulse suddenly felt quite tumultuous. She was relieved that her introduction to Sir Horace relieved her of the necessity of making any sort of reply. Her rather fixed smile relaxed into something more genuine as she glanced at his animated countenance.

"It is a pleasure to make your acquaintance, ma'am. I wish England were as full as it could hold with teachers such as you, for I must tell you that I have recently met three of your pupils; Miss Montagu, Lady Georgianna, and now Miss Fletcher. Dashed fine gals, every one of 'em! Do you proud!"

Amusement danced in her eyes. "I am delighted to hear you think so. But I cannot take all the credit for their characters. They would all have been fine girls with or without my intervention."

She turned to Lord Carstairs. "I must thank you, sir. I have not enjoyed myself so much for a very long time. Now, if you will all excuse me, I must go in. Miss Fletcher will wonder what has become of me. I did not intend to stay out so long."

She had just finished changing when a light knock fell upon her door. Frampton opened it and Charlotte tripped into the room, an excited sparkle in her eyes.

Sarah smiled at her charge. "Well, my dear? I can see you are full of news."

"I am. My cousin is come."

"I know. I have just seen him."

"And did you like him?" she asked eagerly.

"He was certainly all that was polite," she said cautiously.

Charlotte looked a little disappointed but brightened after a moment. "That is not all my news. He brought his friend, Sir Horace, to visit."

"And did *you* like *him?*" Sarah said, interested to hear what her charge had made of such an enthusiastic gentleman.

She laughed. "Yes, very much. There is something about him that is very open and…"

Sarah raised a brow. "And?"

"Well, endearing, I suppose. Although that is a strange way to describe a gentleman."

"Not at all. I have also just made his acquaintance, and think that it is a very apt description. I suppose he told you that he has recently met Marianne and Georgianna?"

The excited glow brightened Charlotte's eyes once more.

"Yes, he told me all about it. He was in Cheltenham with his friend Lord Cranbourne, who is an earl. They met Lady Brancaster, Marianne, and Georgianna at a ball. He said that Lord Cranbourne seemed very taken with Marianne, and has invited them all to his estate in Wiltshire for a house party! Although I had hoped to make my come out with Marianne, would it not be wonderful if she were to become a countess?"

Sarah smiled. "Yes, I suppose it would, for Marianne would never marry if her heart were not engaged. I must admit, I would be curious to meet the man who could capture her heart or put up with her frank ways and unpredictable starts. But do not set any store by this invitation, Charlotte. I would not wish you to be disappointed when she writes to you complaining that he is a stuffed shirt, full of his own importance. Life is not a fairy tale, after all."

Charlotte refused to be cast down. "We shall see. You are sometimes very cynical, Sarah. I believe Sir Horace when he says he has rarely seen his friend behave so well or be so assiduous in his attentions to a young lady."

With that she turned and left the room. Sarah stared after her in stunned silence. After a moment, a broad smile crept across her face. Charlotte's tone had held a hint of censure. This was not the shy, timid girl she had watched over for the past five years. Lady Carstairs' affection had already worked wonders on her confidence. Her forthright manner seemed to be rubbing off on her as well. She firmly ignored the slight sinking feeling in her stomach. She was sure that she was very glad that Charlotte would soon be able to do without her.

CHAPTER 5

A short, rather plump man, with rosy cheeks, stood with his arms outstretched, a coat clasped carefully in his hands. A small frown puckered his brow, and he glanced anxiously at his employer.

"Ahem."

Lord Seymore started and smiled apologetically at his valet.

"I'm sorry, Tench. I was miles away."

"Is it your waistcoat, sir?"

"My waistcoat?" He glanced at the mirror, a puzzled frown furrowing his brow. "I can see nought amiss with my waistcoat."

Tench looked relieved. "I am glad, sir. I chose the plain black this evening as I always think it sets off your claret coat to perfection, as well as being a fitting mark of respect for your aunt."

Lord Seymore looked at his valet in some surprise. "Are you feeling quite the thing, Tench?"

"Yes, sir. It is just that you stood so long staring at your waistcoat in the mirror, I thought that perhaps you did not like it."

"Tench! When have I ever interfered with your sartorial decisions? I pay you a very good wage to make them for me."

His valet sighed. "I hesitate to contradict you, sir, but you interfered when I presented the beautiful silk waistcoat with the exquisitely em-broidered pink flowers."

Lord Seymore gave a shout of laughter. "I should think I did."

"And you refused point blank to wear the yellow and blue striped Petersham trousers."

"They were ridiculous!"

"But there was nothing objectionable about the green——"

"Enough, Tench! If you wished to turn me into a tulip, you must have realised long ago that your ambition was destined to fail."

"Not a tulip, sir," Tench protested. "His tailor makes the tulip, but you, sir, make your tailor. You would give distinction to anything you wore."

His words were not delivered in an obsequious manner, but with a sincere simplicity, as if they were a statement of fact rather than an opinion.

Lord Seymore smiled, not unsympathetically, at his valet. "I must be a sore trial to you, Tench. I am surprised you did not leave my employ years ago and find someone else who would give you an opportunity to display your artistry."

Tench shrugged. "There would be no point, sir. It is rare to come across a gentleman with both an excellent figure and an even temper. You have never once thrown a boot at my head because you have imagined there was a thumbprint on it, threatened to turn me off when your neckcloth was not starched quite to your liking, or boxed my ears because you have discovered a crease in your coat. In short, sir, you are an excellent master."

He picked up Lord Seymore's discarded clothes and bowed. "If that is all, sir?"

"That is more than enough, I think," he said dryly.

As the door to his dressing room shut behind his valet, he again looked in the mirror. But it was not himself he saw, but a pair of slightly defiant green eyes.

He had looked forward to renewing his acquaintance with Miss Hayes. The gentle, modest lady that both Miss Wolfraston and Charlotte had described to him, did not tally with the vital, spirited creature he remembered. He had wondered if he had been so besotted with her when a very green boy, that he had exaggerated her allure over time. He had fully expected to discover that his memory had been at fault. And so it had proved. She was far more beautiful than he recalled.

Just as a portrait, no matter how expertly executed, rarely captured the spark of life that revealed the essence of its subject, so his memory had dulled the pearly luminescence of her smooth skin, the plump lusciousness of her lips, and the clarity of her eyes. They reminded him of the cool, turquoise waters where the shallow, sandy-bottomed sea met a wooded cliff.

When she had ridden into the stable yard with all the confidence and poise that he associated with her, it was as is if the years had rolled back. For an instant, he was a green boy once more. His breath had caught in his throat, and his heart had beaten a little faster, but by the time she had dismounted in such a bold and unusual manner, he was himself again.

If he had not known for a certainty that she had spent the last few years of her life teaching in a seminary, he would never have suspected it. He felt very sorry for her; Turnbull was a cad to leave her in such a position. But although he still admired her beauty, and felt a debt of gratitude towards her for her unremitting care of Charlotte, he was not so grateful that he would consider offering for her. He no longer had any ambition to align himself with such a magnificent creature; he was almost certain Miss Hayes would not make a comfortable wife. He could no more picture her being happy almost permanently ensconced in the countryside, than he could imagine himself able to bear the rigours of the season.

As he descended the stairs, he heard himself hailed from below. Glancing down, he saw the white hair and twinkling blue eyes of Lord Carstairs.

"Join me in the library, Lord Seymore. There are a few minutes yet before we need join the ladies in the drawing room."

He followed him into the east wing, his eyes crinkling in amusement when Lord Carstairs put his finger to his lips as they passed the drawing room. He opened a door further along the corridor and politely waved Lord Seymore to precede him.

Lord Seymore strolled into the library. He liked the room immediately. A huge fireplace dominated the centre of the wall immediately opposite him. A welcoming fire flickered in the wide grate. Large leather armchairs sat on either side of it, and a huge coat of arms bearing an eagle with outspread wings, hung above it. The walls were lined with shelves from floor to ceiling, and some of the volumes that filled them appeared to be quite ancient. Rich ruby curtains covered the windows and a thick carpet covered the floor. It was decorated with brightly coloured swirling patterns. It took a moment for Lord Seymore to pick out the animals that had been artfully woven into the fabric, but slowly the elephants, tigers, and peacocks began to emerge.

"It is wonderful, isn't it?" Lord Carstairs sighed. "I had to leave behind so many beautiful things, but at least this could be rolled up and transported easily."

"I take it you enjoyed your time in India, sir?"

"Oh yes, more than enjoyed it. It became a part of me. I went hoping to make a fortune, as have so many. But the country and its people soon seduced me. Not in a sordid way you understand, although I am sorry to say I witnessed many who did fall into such foolishness. I found the native populations' ways fascinating, and always held to the belief that they must be taken into account when administering justice. I was very fortunate that I rose to a position where I could ensure that this was so. But don't start me blabbering on about that or we will be here all evening. Please, take a seat."

Lord Seymore settled himself in one of the comfortable wingback chairs by the fireplace.

"Your diligence, sir, is to be admired. Would I be correct in assuming that it prevented you from making your fortune?"

Lord Carstairs chuckled. "Indeed you would. A young man when he first arrives in India has many expenses and little income. I, as did many before me, fell into the trap of borrowing money. The interest rates are shocking, and I have seen many foolish men never recover and die in poverty. I soon realised that borrowing was a fool's game, however, but still it took me a few years to recover. And it was no bad thing, after all; it gave me a greater appreciation of the many difficulties the local population face on a daily basis."

Lord Seymore smiled. "I think you should

share this wisdom with Sir Horace. His brother seems set on teaching him a similar lesson."

"Really? Well Mr Bamber is a very good sort. If he thinks Sir Horace would benefit from such a lesson, then I am sure he is right. But perhaps I should not comment, for I came back from India a very wealthy man after all."

"You must have been very competent to rise to the rank of judge so I am in sure you deserved the rewards."

Lord Carstairs chuckled. "My position made me very comfortable, but it was Augusta who made me rich. She is a very remarkable woman."

Lord Seymore's brows rose. "I was aware that Lady Carstairs' former employer had left her a gift in her will that enabled her to travel to India, but I had no idea she was left a fortune."

"She was not. But she watched with increasing contempt the way so many of our countrymen and women tried to create their little corner of England in the country. They yearned for everything British and so she obliged them. She saw their extravagance and foolishness as an opportunity. She would never have countenanced exploiting the locals, but she saw no harm in taking advantage of what she called the interlopers. She started importing everything from furniture, fabric, and hats, to wine, china, and coffee. She learned Persian, Hindustani, and Bengali, and developed a network of Indian contacts to transport them to wherever there was an English settlement."

"That is certainly an impressive achievement. And you did not mind your wife being involved in trade, sir?"

"Why should I? Remember, I was only Mr Fancot then, and we were a long way from home. It would not do now, of course. But I am sure Augusta will find another project. She does not like to be idle."

Lord Seymore smiled. "I take it Charlotte is her latest project?"

"Oh, she is much more than that. We are both very fond of her already. She is a delightful girl. Lady Carstairs has approached me about setting up a trust for her."

"That is very generous of you, sir. Charlotte is also the main beneficiary of my late aunt's will. She is rapidly becoming a wealthy young lady."

"Is that so? I was under the impression that apart from yourself, Charlotte was friendless."

"I am afraid that is true," he said ruefully. "My aunt was not always in the best of health and did not feel she could offer any support to my ward. This preyed on her mind, and it seems her guilt drove her to this last generous act."

"You do not seem troubled by this redemptive gesture, Lord Seymore, yet you might reasonably have expected to benefit yourself."

Lord Seymore shrugged. "I am wealthy enough. It could make little difference to me, and although Charlotte is far from penniless, it can only improve her chances of achieving a respectable marriage."

"Please excuse me for interrupting, but Lady Carstairs asked me to remind you that it is nearly the dinner hour and she would be pleased if you would join the ladies in the drawing room."

Neither gentleman had heard Mr Fancot enter the room.

Lord Carstairs got to his feet. "We will continue this discussion another time, Lord Seymore."

He turned to his steward and grinned. "I will lay odds, Charles, she did not frame her request in quite that manner."

"Perhaps not, sir. But I have accurately interpreted the gist of her message if not the tone in which it was delivered."

"What used to lay here?" Lord Seymore asked.

He had been drawn to a lectern that was carved in the form of an eagle. Its clawed feet formed the base, and its outstretched wings the top. A book of some sort had clearly lain there for a long time, as the wood in the centre was far darker than around the edges.

Lord Carstairs frowned. "It was a book that contained the history of the family. It is the duty of whoever is head of the family to keep it updated. It contains the family tree, of course, but also snippets of interest about my ancestors, including both their achievements and their foolishness. It is meant as a sort of guide. It has always lain there. It is kept in a leather box with a lock. Only the current earl is permitted to hold the key. It would not do for anyone to discover the skeletons in our closet after all. When I came home, I found the key but the book was gone. Although both Charles and I have searched high and low, we have not been able to find it. It is a puzzle." His expression cleared. "I am sure it will turn up sooner or later. This room was repainted just before I returned; someone probably put it out of harm's way and then forgot all about it."

As soon as they entered the drawing room, Lady Carstairs rose to her feet and crossed the room to her husband. "At last. Take me into dinner, at once, Carstairs, for I am famished."

He kissed her hand before placing it on his arm. "Of course, my dear. It would not do to have you fainting away."

"I have never fainted in my life, Carstairs, as well you know. Wouldn't dream of doing such a thing." She glanced over her shoulder as he led her towards the door. "Mr Fancot, you may take Charlotte in."

Lord Seymore offered his arm to Sarah. "Miss Hayes?"

She hesitated for a moment before laying her fingers very lightly on his arm. A rather awkward silence hung between them. Lord Seymore was the first to break it.

"I have not yet had the opportunity to thank you for all you have done for Charlotte."

Her gaze remained fixed firmly ahead. "It is quite unnecessary, Lord Seymore. I was only doing my job, after all."

"I think, ma'am, that your many small kindnesses to my ward, went far beyond the strict obligations of duty."

She glanced quickly up at him for the briefest moment. Lord Seymore's brows rose. He saw both disapproval and condemnation writ clear in her eyes. She may as well have accused him outright of having failed to do more himself.

He was relieved that she turned her attentions to Lord Carstairs once they were seated, for he could not defend himself when she had not spoken the words aloud. His lips twisted into a grimace. His only line of argument would have been that Charlotte had not wished to be removed from the seminary, preferring the company of Miss Hayes to his own. And whilst that might have been true, it had also been the course of least resistance.

His eyes rose to his ward and he was aware of a feeling of pride as he watched her converse with Mr Fancot. Her manners were all they should be. She seemed a little more reserved than she had been with Sir Horace, but answered him with composure when addressed.

"It must be a sore trial to you, Lord Seymore."

He turned to Lady Carstairs in surprise. "I'm sorry, ma'am?"

"To be afflicted with deafness so young."

His eyes creased in amusement. "Forgive me, ma'am. I don't know where my manners have gone begging. What was it you wished to say to me?"

"I asked if you had an opinion on sea bathing."

"I find it very invigorating, ma'am," he said, smiling. "Winbourne is very close to the coast, and I often go for a dip in the summer."

"Good. Then you won't object to Charlotte testing the waters at Weymouth."

He quirked a brow. "Have you ever been sea bathing in England, ma'am?"

"I have not. However, I do believe one should try new things, especially those on offer locally."

Lord Seymore glanced over at Charlotte. As Lady Carstairs' voice tended to carry to every corner of a room, he was not surprised to see her following their conversation.

"Well, Charlotte? Do you think you would enjoy it? I warn you, sea water is very cold."

She looked a little uncertain. "I cannot swim."

"I have made some enquiries," Lady Carstairs said. "You need not go out of your depth, my dear. And if you are worried about your modesty you need not be. I believe you change in a closed wagon, which is then pulled into the sea by a horse. Male and female bathing is kept strictly separate, of course."

Charlotte looked across at Sarah. "Will you come, Miss Hayes?"

"Most certainly I will," she said. "We had a lake on our estate and my father taught me to swim when I was a child. The sensation of cool water rushing over your skin is quite wonderful. I used to enjoy floating on the surface whilst I watched the clouds scud across the sky. The feeling of weightlessness is quite remarkable." She turned to Lady Carstairs. "It is an excellent notion, ma'am. Will you go in?"

Lady Carstairs gave her a look of approval. "Of course I shall. Did I not say I like to try new things?"

"It seems I can have nothing to say in the matter," Lord Seymore said dryly, firmly banishing the image of Miss Hayes drifting on the water, her unbound hair floating about her.

"Will you come?" Charlotte asked.

"Yes," he said. He glanced at Lady Carstairs. "I will ask Sir Horace if you don't mind, ma'am? I am sure he will be grateful for the diversion."

"The more the merrier." she said. "Carstairs?"

"I think not, my dear. If I were meant to swim, I would have gills. And considering how much you dislike the cold, I am not at all sure you will enjoy it, Augusta." He smiled gently at her. "However, I know that once you get a bee in your bonnet there is no stopping you, so I shall not try to dissuade you."

He turned to Mr Fancot. "If you wish to go, Charles, please feel free."

He smiled deprecatingly. "I think I am as one with you, sir, on this matter. Besides, I wish to oversee the digging of the new drainage system in the west field."

"I do not know what I would do without you, Charles. We really should consider getting you some help. After all, this will all be yours when I am gone. You should be socialising more and working less. You should think about finding a wife. My brother should have done his duty and married, of course, but he always was a bit of a rum touch. Never did understand him really."

Charles gave an understanding smile. "He could be quite crusty, sir, but he was always very generous towards me. As for marriage, there's time enough yet, and I'm quite happy in my current role. Indeed, I would be very reluctant to give it up."

"As you wish. But perhaps when your mother's year of mourning is up you will change your mind. I know you do not like to leave her alone.

I am glad that you, at least, have started supping with us of an evening."

"You are indeed a very conscientious and fond son," Lady Carstairs said. "I must pay Mrs Fancot a visit and try again to persuade her to also take her dinner with us. I have invited the vicar and his brother to join us tomorrow evening; her presence would even up the numbers a trifle."

"You are very kind, ma'am."

"If you're off sea bathing you will need to leave early, my dear," Lord Carstairs said, "so leave it to me."

CHAPTER 6

Sir Horace jumped at the chance to escape his brother's clutches. He must have been keeping a weather eye out for his liberator, for no sooner had Lord Seymore pulled up outside the parsonage, with the barouche following close behind, than he came hurtling down the path with more haste than grace.

"I think Loftus is touched in his upper works, Seymore," he said. "My valet thinks so too. He brought me a pair of rough brown trousers and some sort of smock thing this morning. When I told Loftus the joke was wearing thin, he assured me it was no jest. Said he did not wish me to damage any of my fine clothes whilst I chopped the wood!"

He paused to doff his hat and bow to the ladies as the barouche pulled up.

"I am glad to see you are so punctual, Sir Horace," Lady Carstairs said, an amused glint in her eyes. "You are clearly very eager to take your exercise. I shall look forward to hearing how you enjoyed your swim."

His mouth twisted into something halfway between a smile and a grimace. "Well, as to that, ma'am. Thought I might just enjoy a stroll along the esplanade."

"We will all enjoy a stroll along the esplanade," she assured him.

He looked relieved.

"After we have all enjoyed a dip," she added firmly.

His face fell.

"Come, man. Even Charlotte, who is a little afraid of the water, is going to go in."

His glance swivelled in her direction and he straightened his shoulders as she smiled shyly at him.

"I think it only fair that you try it as well, Sir Horace," she said gently. "Then we can compare notes afterwards."

He bowed elegantly. "Your wish is my command, Miss Fletcher. The thought that such a delicate creature as yourself is enduring—"

Lady Carstairs raised her brows.

"I meant to say, *enjoying* the experience at the same moment as myself, will bolster my resolve, I am sure."

"But a great distance away," Lady Carstairs said dryly.

Sir Horace coloured. "Of course, ma'am, I did not meant to imply, that is—"

"Come along, Bamber," Lord Seymore said. "You must not keep my horses waiting."

He sent a grateful look in the direction of his friend. "No, of course not. Sorry, old chap."

As the curricle pulled away, Charlotte stifled a giggle.

"Buffoon!" Lady Carstairs muttered.

"Oh, do not say so," Charlotte protested. "I like him."

"You do?" she said surprised.

Charlotte nodded. "Yes. I think he is very sweet."

"Really? Well, perhaps I was a little harsh. But if he goes into the water above his knees, I will own myself astonished!"

Lady Carstairs read them snippets from the guidebook she had acquired as they approached Weymouth.

"You will be pleased to hear, Charlotte, that

the bay is so well protected from the winds that the sea is remarkably tranquil."

As they drove along the seafront they discovered the truth of this assertion. The day was fine and the water glimmered turquoise in the shallows. Hardly a wave disturbed its even surface, and it lapped softly against the shore in gentle invitation. Rows of sea bathing machines, each with a brightly painted roof, dotted the golden sand. The squeal of the seagulls gracefully gliding further out to sea, were echoed by the shrieks of the bathers as they submerged themselves in the water for the first time.

Sarah shared a bathing hut with Charlotte. She changed quickly into her flannel bathing shift before helping Charlotte into hers.

Once the hut had been pulled far enough into the water, she opened the door and shook her head at the two women who were waiting in case she needed their assistance. They moved aside and she executed a neat, shallow dive into the sea.

"Is it very cold?" asked Charlotte, eyeing it certainly.

"Yes," Sarah admitted, rolling onto her back and sculling with her hands. "But only for a moment."

Charlotte slowly lowered herself in,

squealing and laughing as the water rose inch by inch up her body.

"It is better to enter swiftly," Sarah said.

"I believe you are right, Miss Hayes," Lady Carstairs agreed, emerging from the hut next to them.

She clutched the skirt of her shift in one hand, took a deep breath, and leapt feet first into the sea.

Charlotte gasped as her aunt lost her footing and momentarily disappeared beneath the gentle swell. Sarah tried to stand, but her billowing shift slowed the process and by the time her feet found purchase in the firm sand, Lady Carstairs had burst through the ripples, a wide grin creasing her dripping face.

"Cold!" she cried. "It is positively Arctic!"

The next moment, they were all clutching hands and laughing.

Lady Carstairs had done Sir Horace an injustice when she had suggested he was not likely to allow the water to go above his knees. Although it was true he liked his creature comforts, once Sir Horace had committed to something, he always followed through.

She would also have been very surprised to see that although his figure was not as well defined as Lord Seymore's, it was very trim and lean muscles rippled in his arms as he cut through the water with remarkable ease.

After a brisk swim they floated in the warmer shallows for a while.

"You are a fraud, Bamber," said his friend. "Why such a show of reluctance when you are such a competent swimmer?"

"I am no such thing, Seymore. I never said I couldn't swim, but I learned in the warm waters of the Mediterranean, old chap."

"Of course. I had forgotten that you travelled to Greece and Turkey."

"Those were the days," Sir Horace said, a little wistfully. "There were so many fascinating ruins to explore. Meant to go to Egypt as well, but my father died and I had to come home. My mother was so cast down it seemed heartless to go off again. The waters there are crystal clear, and when you swim it is like taking a warm bath. I must admit that I did not relish the thought of immersing myself in our English waters. But I must say, that after the initial shock, they are really quite refreshing."

"Where else do you take your exercise? I have never seen you box at Jackson's."

"I don't. Can't say I enjoy the sport. Cranbourne, my neighbour, is very keen on it."

"Yes, I know. I've enjoyed more than one encounter with him."

"I will never understand why you all enjoy pummelling each other so much. He's given me private lessons, mind you. Insisted on it. Said I'd be the perfect target for footpads. I've never had to put them into practice, thank heavens."

"Then how do you explain your fitness?"

"I often tramp across the countryside for miles when I am at home. Quite interested in birds, actually. And I enjoy riding as much as the next man. Just as well because I'm terrible at handling the ribbons. Completely ham-fisted. I've had to have two curricles repaired. Drove one into a farmer's cart – dashed bad business – turnips all over the road, and the other into a tree when trying to avoid some madcap young scamp who had taken charge of a stagecoach."

Lord Seymour laughed and splashed his friend playfully. "Even so, you're a bit of a dark horse, Bamber."

There followed a brief and thoroughly undignified bout of horseplay as they dived upon one another as if they were mortal enemies intent on drowning their victim.

"Don't mean to be," Sir Horace gasped,

when they called a truce. "Not the sort of things you talk about over a game of cards at your club. To be honest, I'd spend a lot more time in the country if my mother wouldn't insist I accompany her to Town for the season, and would desist from inviting a succession of unfortunate relatives to catch my interest during the summer."

Lord Seymore smiled at him sympathetically. "Come on, Bamber. We don't want to keep Lady Carstairs waiting."

They met the ladies on the esplanade.

"Well, Sir Horace? Enjoy your swim?" Lady Carstairs asked, eyeing his damp hair.

"Thoroughly, ma'am." He turned to Charlotte and offered her his arm. "Care to compare those notes?"

Lord Seymore strolled between Miss Hayes and Lady Carstairs.

"So he did go in then?" Lady Carstairs said, as Charlotte and Sir Horace fell a little behind.

"Swam like a fish, ma'am. But he prefers the waters in warmer climes."

"Oh? He has travelled then?"

"Quite extensively I believe, ma'am. He's fascinated by archaeology."

She stared at him in some astonishment. "I

see I shall have to have a conversation with Sir Horace after dinner this evening."

"Wait a moment," Miss Hayes said suddenly, glancing over her shoulder. "I cannot see Charlotte."

Lord Seymore could not fail to detect the note of anxiety in her voice. "Do not worry, Miss Hayes, I am sure she will be quite safe in the company of Sir Horace."

He realised that he was not merely offering her comfort; he really believed it. He was beginning to realise that beneath all his dandifying, and his sometimes naïve remarks, lay hidden depths. He seemed malleable, yet he had not meekly succumbed to his mother's matchmaking efforts or his brother's strong-arm tactics.

The esplanade was full of people taking the air and Sir Horace and Charlotte were not immediately apparent in the crowd, but Lord Seymore had the advantage of height and soon spotted them. They had moved over to the edge of the walkway to converse with two thin, rather plain looking women. Knowing his friend's tendency to forget the names of many of the ladies he was introduced to, he sincerely hoped he was not about to cause him any embarrassment.

He need not have worried. Much to Lady Bamber's despair, in his efforts to avoid having to stand up with the many young hopefuls who thronged a ballroom, Sir Horace had cultivated the acquaintance of a range of ladies who, due to their situation, age, or inclination, did not often dance. Thus, he relieved himself of the excruciating embarrassment of stepping on another fair maiden's toes, not to mention the herculean effort of trying to keep up a coherent conversation whilst he endeavoured to remember the steps.

He glanced up as they approached and introduced Lady Turnbull and Miss Lavenham. Lord Seymore could not help glancing down at Miss Hayes to see her reaction. He thought he detected a look of surprise in her eyes but it was swiftly gone and she appeared to be quite composed.

"I have been advised to take the waters for my health," Lady Turnbull informed them. "I have been a little under the weather of late."

Her air of extreme fragility and the dark shadows under her eyes confirmed her assertion.

"And do you think they are doing you some good?" asked Lady Carstairs.

"Yes, I have been here a week now and feel so much improved I think I may attend a ball at the assembly rooms on Friday." She smiled gently at Sir Horace. "Might you consider attending? I always enjoy our little chats at such events."

Sir Horace coloured. "Would be delighted, ma'am, but I'm staying near Dorchester with my brother, you know, and the thing is I have no transport."

Lady Turnbull accepted this excuse meekly and turned to her rather stern looking companion. "Never mind, I have Miss Lavenham to keep me company."

They took their leave and soon disappeared into the crowd.

"Aunt Augusta?" Charlotte said gently.

Lady Carstairs stood unmoving, her gaze fixed on the sea and her thoughts seemingly far away.

"You shall go to the ball, Sir Horace," she suddenly exclaimed.

His eyes widened in alarm. "No! I mean, that is to say, there's no need—"

Her penetrating gaze swivelled in his direction. "There is every need. Charlotte cannot remain hidden away at Priddleton Hall all summer. It is time she spread her wings a little."

"But, Aunt, there is plenty of time yet, surely? I am trying new things. Today I went in the sea, and Sir Horace has offered to teach me to ride if you have a suitable horse in the stables. Is that not enough, for now?"

"Oh, he has, has he? Well that is a very good start; you may wish to ride in the park in Town. But I am still of the opinion that you should go to the ball. You will have the advantage of three partners that you already know; Carstairs, Lord Seymore, and Sir Horace."

"But you do not enjoy polite social gatherings, Aunt."

"All the more reason for us to go. I cannot bring you out without going to a host of the things. I may as well become accustomed sooner as later."

"But, ma'am, I am a terrible dancer!" Sir Horace exclaimed. He glanced at Charlotte and his colour heightened. "If I had to dance, I am sure there is no one I would as lief stand up with than you, Miss Fletcher, but I make a hash of it every time."

"Well, you have six days to improve," Lady Carstairs pointed out.

Charlotte could not bear to see Sir Horace so alarmed. She put her hand gently on his arm. "We will strike a bargain. You will teach me to ride, and in turn, I shall help you practice your dancing. You will play for us won't you, Miss Hayes?"

"Of course," she murmured, a little distractedly.

"Well, that is settled then," Lady Carstairs said. "You may as well come and stay at the hall, Sir Horace. Between the riding lessons and the dancing practice you will be there most of the time, anyway. Besides, you are bound to run out of ways to avoid all those little tasks your brother has lined up for you, if you don't. I do not wish to hear that you still cannot dance because you were too busy feeding the chickens to practice!"

Sir Horace's face brightened. "I say, ma'am, that's dashed kind of you."

CHAPTER 7

S arah somehow managed to keep up a meaningless flow of conversation during the drive back to Priddleton Hall, but she was very grateful to escape to her room for a warm bath before it was time to dress for dinner.

She lay back, closed her eyes, and tried to relax the tense muscles that clenched her shoulders. She had spent the last few years trying to rigorously control her life. She had planned her lessons, given extra succour to any of her pupils who needed it, especially Charlotte, and deputised for Miss Wolfraston whenever she had been indisposed. She had not allowed herself to think much beyond that. She had ensured that her days were so busy that she had little time for reflection.

But now, things seemed to be slipping away from her. The decision to accompany Charlotte had opened the door to a host of unforeseen consequences. First, she had bumped into Lord Turnbull. Then she had had to face Lord Seymore. He had not indicated to either Miss Wolfraston or Charlotte that he intended to join them in Dorset. Considering his sporadic visits to his ward, she had not considered it at all likely. She had thought it far more probable that he would see Lady Carstairs' invitation as an excuse to abdicate all responsibility for her.

The encounter with Lord Turnbull should have been the most disturbing by far, yet strangely it was not. Once her anger at his disgraceful behaviour had passed, she had felt relief that she had not permanently aligned herself with the man. She was in no doubt that he had been, and still was, attracted to both her physical appearance and her spirit, but she was equally sure that he had never loved her.

She had felt a deep and abiding love for her father, and would have done anything to help him if she had known that he had been in such dire straits. She would certainly never have allowed him to squander such vast amounts on her come out. The irony was, that she had never been happier than when she had been at home with him. She could not deny that she had been dazzled by the life and gaiety of the metropolis, but it had never been her ambition to cut a figure there; the ambition had been all her father's, and she had never liked to disappoint him.

Her reaction to Lord Seymore was far more disturbing because it was both contradictory and hypocritical. He had barely made an impression upon her when she had first met him, but it would be useless to deny that she felt a strange and unwelcome tug of attraction to him now.

At first, she had only acknowledged to herself that the years had enhanced his youthful good looks. But when she had laid her hand on his sleeve yesterday, she had felt her fingers tingle, even though it was the lightest of touches. She had tried to put it down to the anger she had long felt towards the man who could and should have provided Charlotte with a home. The excuse that a single man could know no better held no water with her. Her father had not baulked at the task of bringing up a young girl on his own. She acknowledged that the circumstances were different; the ties were not so close – but the principle was the same.

Yet when she had walked next to Lord Seymore along the esplanade in Weymouth, although she had hardly heard a word he had uttered, she had been fully aware of his presence. She did not understand why she should feel this awkward physical attraction towards the man who she had long held in some contempt. She knew, of course, that Charlotte had requested to stay at the seminary, but he had made no serious attempt to dissuade her. Or had he? Having absented herself from all their meetings she could not be sure. Charlotte clearly felt some affection for him. He had visited her three times a year and regularly corresponded with her between those visits, so perhaps this was not surprising.

A small frown puckered her brow as she absentmindedly stroked the bar of rose soap along her arm. He was not as she had imagined him to be. His manner was assured, charming, and relaxed, but then had not Lord Turnbull also been charming? She opened her eyes and sighed. He had also been restless, often outrageous, and quite scathing about those he did not admire. She had found his maliciously witty comments amusing.

She had not been proud of that once she'd recovered from her infatuation, especially as his remarks had often been aimed at the more plain young ladies in search of a husband, or the more eccentric old tabbies who would not hesitate to cross swords with him. She felt sorry for the poor dab of a creature who had become his wife. She could only imagine that she was wealthy.

If Lord Turnbull had needed a rich wife, no wonder he had been relieved when she had released him from his obligation. She would have been grateful, however, if he had explained as much to her; it might have saved her some humiliation, at least. But whilst she could understand that his circumstances may have made it provident for him to marry a woman of substance, his subsequent behaviour was contemptible. Lady Turnbull had not looked at all well, and whilst she was attempting to restore her failing health, her husband was squandering her money at the races, getting inebriated, and forcing his attentions on his old flame. She had made a poor bargain.

Lord Turnbull would have disparaged Lady Carstairs, she was sure. Yet Lord Seymore's eyes lit up with amusement at her abrupt and often quite rude comments. Neither did he seem to object to the peremptory way in which she expected them all to fall in with her plans. Lord Turnbull would never have agreed to do anything he had not wished to. He had been quite selfish.

She had attached this flaw to Lord Seymore, but she was no longer quite so confident that it was true. Not only had he made the journey into Dorset to ensure that Charlotte was happy with her great aunt, but he seemed inclined to remain and further his relationship with his ward, as well as develop an acquaintance with her relatives. She had, she realised, somehow intertwined her own sense of abandonment by Lord Turnbull, with Charlotte's abandonment by Lord Seymore. But he had not really deserted her and the cases were quite different.

She grimaced as she realised the water had turned cold. Frampton poked her head around the screen

"Come on, miss, you'll be late down if we don't hurry."

As she stood, she came to a decision. She must allow her prejudice to slide from her, even as the water now slid from her body. She would begin again with Lord Seymore, for Charlotte's sake as well as her own. As for her attraction to him, it would be a passing thing, she was sure. She certainly could not hide from him here as she had at the seminary. Her brow cleared. It was hardly surprising that she should find herself attracted to him. He could have been anyone. It had been a long time since she had spent time in the company of a handsome man, or any man for that matter. He just happened to be the first one who had crossed her path – sober, at least. The more she saw of him the less he would affect her. Did not Shakespeare mention in one of his plays that a surfeit of something makes the appetite for it sicken and so die?

With this in mind, she smiled warmly at Lord Seymore when he bowed to her as she entered the drawing room.

His eyebrows rose. "Good evening, Miss Hayes. I am pleased to see you in such good spirits."

"Have I seemed such a crosspatch, sir?"

He smiled gently. "I would not go so far, ma'am. But I did have the feeling that perhaps you disapproved of me."

Sarah felt a spurt of annoyance. Did the man have to be so forthright? She might be offering him an olive branch, but she had no desire to open her heart to him.

"It is not my place to approve or disapprove of you, Lord Seymore," she said, a little stiffly.

He frowned, but said calmly, "If you do not wish to air your grievances against me, I shall respect your wishes, ma'am. But please do not hide behind your position. It is disingenuous and unworthy of you. I am very sorry that your father's death put you in such an unfortunate position, but we both know that your birth is noble. Even if it were not, I do not see why a companion or teacher should not be allowed to speak equally as frankly as the person she is talking to."

This encounter was not going quite as Sarah had intended. She felt relieved when Sir Horace and Mr Bamber were announced. Again her expectations of a gentleman were confounded. Lady Carstairs had shared the list of things Mr Bamber had drawn up for his brother, and she had formed in her mind the image of a very severe man. He certainly dressed far more soberly than his brother, as befitted a man of the cloth, and he had a long, thin, intelligent face. But his eyes, which were the same moss green as his brother's, held a definite glimmer of humour when he spoke with her.

"Miss Hayes, I am very pleased to make your acquaintance. My mother would also be very happy to meet you, I suspect."

He surprised a laugh out of her. "And why is that, sir?"

"She despairs of ever getting my brother to the altar. He has always been extremely uncomfortable around young ladies and generally avoids them whenever possible. But he has now

met three who he cannot praise highly enough —
all of them pupils of yours."

Her eyes turned in Sir Horace's direction for
a moment and she saw that he was happily ensconced in conversation with Charlotte.

"I must take your word for it as I have never
witnessed any awkwardness between him and
Miss Fletcher. But I cannot in all good con-
science take the credit for his change of heart. It
is perhaps because all of the girls you refer to,
are very young and not yet out, and so he feels
safe to converse with them."

"As you say, but I think it not outside of the
realms of possibility that when he goes up to
Town for the season, next year, he will not be
quite so averse to cultivating the acquaintance of
the fairer sex."

"I hope you may be right, sir." His friendly
manner encouraged her to speak aloud the
thoughts that were uppermost in her mind. "I
must admit that I am a little surprised that you
do not seem at all put out that he has decamped
to the hall before he could have had time to ac-
complish any of the *extraordinary* tasks you set
him."

She was surprised to see a rather wolfish grin
cross the vicar's face. "What a strange impression I must have given you, Miss Hayes. I will

admit that I was punishing him, just a little, and also following a course of action which I was sure my mother would approve of."

He chuckled as he saw her astonishment. "Now you will think we are all barking mad. Let me explain. My brother slunk off to Cheltenham claiming he had a bad case of gout in his left foot. It was a complete fabrication of course; he just wished to avoid the latest stray female my mother had invited to stay. He then came to visit me in case she was still there."

Sarah smiled. "I see. You thought to punish him for his deceit, and at the same time make him so uncomfortable that he might go home, after all. That a vicar should be so devious quite alarms me, Mr Bamber."

"Shocking, isn't it?" he agreed cheerfully.

"But you have failed in both of your objectives, and so perhaps have got your just deserts?"

His grin widened. "God moves in mysterious ways, Miss Hayes. Not only is Horace cultivating a friendship with a lady, he is also determined to finally improve his execrable dancing, and means to attend a ball! My mother would be dancing a jig if she knew."

She laughed. "Is his dancing really that bad?"

"Yes!"

"Oh dear. I see Charlotte has set herself a difficult task. He, in turn, has offered to teach her to ride. Ought I let him?"

"You need have no fears on that head, ma'am. He rides very well, but for heaven's sake, don't allow him near a curricle!"

They both glanced up as two new arrivals were announced. It appeared that Lord Carstairs' powers of persuasion were greater than his wife's. Mr Fancot had his mother on his arm. She was quite diminutive, very slender, and wore a rather fine dress of black silk. A thick veil hung from her hat obscuring her face. Sarah was surprised she could see where she was going. Mr Fancot led her to a chair. Once seated, she un-hurriedly untied the ribbons of her bonnet and removed it.

Sarah knew a moment's surprise. If she had not known that she must be at least in her late forties to have a son Mr Fancot's age, she would never have guessed it. Hardly a wisp of grey dis-turbed her midnight dark hair, and only the finest of lines marred her smooth skin. Her eyes were large in her heart-shaped face, and of the softest, deepest brown. They rested for a mo-ment on each member of the party as they were introduced to her, and her voice when she greeted them was barely more than a whisper.

Mr Bamber bowed to Sarah. "I have long wished to make the acquaintance of Mrs Fancot, but she is something of a recluse and does not even come to church. Perhaps I can change her mind, so if you will excuse me?"

"Of course. I would not wish to keep you from such a worthy endeavour."

She found Lord Seymore at her elbow. He smiled disarmingly at her. "I apologise if I was ungracious earlier. Shall we start again?"

"There is nothing to apologise for, sir," she said, not quite meeting his gaze.

A heavy silence fell between them and she did not know quite how to break it.

"You and the vicar seemed to be very pleased with each other," Lord Seymore finally said.

She glanced quickly up at him, but relaxed when she saw no hint of criticism in his eyes. "Did we? We were talking about Sir Horace."

She explained the vicar's motivations concerning his brother, and saw his eyes deepen with amusement.

"Poor Bamber. I really think they should leave him to his own devices. A man should not be manipulated in such a fashion."

"Perhaps not," she conceded. "But they have his best interests at heart, I am sure."

She looked over to where she had last seen him, but it was Mr Fancot who now stood talking to Charlotte. Her eyes were downcast and her shoulders very slightly hunched. She was clearly uncomfortable.

"Excuse me, Lord Seymore. I have just remembered something I wished to say to Charlotte."

She moved swiftly across the room to her charge. "Mr Fancot," she said, smiling. "I am so sorry to interrupt, but I must just have a quick word with Miss Fletcher. Do you mind?"

She thought she saw a flash of irritation in his eyes, but she may have been mistaken, for it was gone in an instant.

"Not at all, Miss Hayes. We can continue our conversation at dinner."

As he bowed and moved away, she turned her clear gaze on Charlotte.

"What has Mr Fancot said to put you all on end?"

Charlotte shook her head. "Nothing really. He was very complimentary. He told me that I reminded him of a fresh daisy. He said that I had a beauty that was no less potent for being chaste and modest, and just like the little unassuming flower could brighten a patch of grass, so I brought a ray of sunshine into the gloomiest of rooms."

Sarah's brows winged up. "How very presumptuous of him."

Charlotte looked uncertain. "Was it? I do not know. I am not used to such talk. But it was not only his words that made me uncomfortable. There is something about him that makes me feel a little afraid. It is his eyes, I think. Have you noticed how intently he looks at you when he talks to you? It is like he is trying to look into your very soul."

"I think that is just his natural expression, and we can hardly blame him for that," Sarah said. "But do not worry, my dear. I shall just pop out and have a quick word with Riddle. I will ask him to exchange our places. You will then be next to Sir Horace. Would that make you more comfortable?"

Charlotte's eyes widened. "Yes, but I do not wish to cause any trouble."

Sarah gave her a reassuring smile. "There will be no trouble. Mr Fancot will perhaps realise that his words were inappropriate, but I am sure no one else will even notice."

If this was not quite true, only Lady Carstairs raised an eyebrow. But Sarah gave her a very speaking look and she merely gave her an almost imperceptible nod in return.

Mr Fancot clearly realised that he had taken a misstep. He toyed with the food on his plate for a few minutes, before glancing quickly around the table.

"I am sorry if I have discomposed Miss Fletcher. It was not my intention," he said in a low voice.

Sarah considered how best to deal with him. He seemed a very worthy young man, and he might be considered to be a very good catch as he was the heir presumptive to Lord Carstairs, but as Charlotte had professed herself to be afraid of him, she would save them both further embarrassment if she discouraged him for the time being, at least. Once Charlotte got a notion into her head, it was sometimes quite difficult to dislodge it.

"She is not used to hearing flowery commonplaces, Mr Fancot."

A dull flush crept along his cheekbones.

"My words were heartfelt, ma'am. She looked so lovely that they were out before I knew what I was about. I should have become better acquainted with her, of course, before they passed my lips—"

"Yes, you should. But even then I think they

would have fallen upon stony ground, sir. She is barely out of the schoolroom and is not yet ready for such attentions from a gentleman."

He glanced across the table and saw Charlotte smiling at something Sir Horace was saying to her.

"She does not seem to mind the attentions of *that* gentleman."

He was clearly a little jealous. Sarah had a feeling that Charlotte might be the first young lady to have engaged his interest. She knew from personal experience how easily young men and women, who were experiencing their first infatuation, could mistake it for something stronger.

"Mr Fancot, it seems you have fallen quite hard for a pretty face. You have my sympathy. But if you imagine yourself in love, you are deluding yourself. You hardly know Miss Fletcher. As for Sir Horace, they are fast developing a friendship, I admit. But it is an innocent friendship. If he were to suddenly utter romantic nonsense to her, she would be no more pleased with him than she was with you. You have frightened the child, and so I would ask you to keep your distance as much as common politeness allows."

The wounded look in the eyes that turned to her, made her soften the blow.

"It may be that if you follow my advice she

will feel more kindly disposed to you, but you must be patient."

As she turned her head, she met Mrs Fancot's gaze. She said nothing and her expression was enigmatic, yet Sarah felt sure she had heard every word.

She was left in no doubt of it later. When the ladies withdrew to the drawing room, whilst Charlotte was talking to Lady Carstairs, Mrs Fancot turned to Sarah, who sat on a chair near her, and said, "I believe you are here as companion to Miss Fletcher?"

"Yes, ma'am. I have, at present, that pleasure."

Mrs Fancot gave a soft laugh. "Pleasure? Come now, Miss Hayes, you may be honest with me. Indeed, I hope that you will be. Let us admit that it is rarely a pleasure to serve others. I was also a companion to a lady before I married Mr Fancot, you see. He had the living here at the time."

Sarah's brows rose. "I had not realised. I was under the impression that your son only came here when he had completed his education."

"Yes," she confirmed. "We moved parish before he was born. I do not wish to speak ill of the dead, Miss Hayes, but the previous Lord Carstairs was of a very different character to the

present one. He was as cold and uncompro-
mising as the current holder of the title is warm
and considerate. My husband and he disagreed
on a number of matters and so when the living
at his other estate, Filton, became free, they
agreed that he should go there."

Mrs Fancot could not quite keep a hint of
bitterness out of her voice.

Sarah offered her a sympathetic smile. "Oh
dear, ma'am. Their disagreements must have
been great indeed."

"Yes," she acknowledged flatly, her eyes
dropping to where her hands lay clenched in
her lap.

Sarah cast about for something to say that
would give Mrs Fancot's thoughts a more posi-
tive turn.

"At least this falling out did not prevent the
late Lord Carstairs from sponsoring your son,
ma'am," she said gently.

Her head snapped up. Her eyes had darkened so that they appeared almost black.

"He could hardly have failed to do so when
there was every likelihood that Charles would
succeed him. Both his brother's age, and the circumstance of him living so long in India, must
have made it increasingly unlikely that he would
live long enough to do so. Therefore, it was only

right, and indeed his duty, to ensure that Charles should understand his lineage and be fully prepared, when the day came, to claim it."

Sarah was quite taken aback by the quiet vehemence of her words.

"You must be very proud of Mr Fancot, ma'am. Lord Carstairs speaks very highly of him."

Her expression softened. "Indeed I am, Miss Hayes. I am also glad that his dedication to his duty is finally being acknowledged as it should be."

"Yes," Sarah smiled. "It is always nice to feel appreciated."

"We have digressed, but that brings me back to the start of our conversation. You are a very confident and self-assured companion, Miss Hayes."

Sarah eyed Mrs Fancot warily. Although the words were softly spoken, some instinct warned her that they were not meant as a compliment.

"Do you think so?" she said carefully. "Perhaps it is my age, ma'am."

"Perhaps," agreed Mrs Fancot. "But I do not think that quite excuses you from speaking to my son in the way you did at dinner. I understand why you gave him such advice, of course."

Sarah coloured slightly and sat a little

straighter. "I hope so, ma'am. I only wished to save both Miss Fletcher and Mr Fancot any further embarrassment."

Mrs Fancot's eyes narrowed. "Indeed? As Miss Fletcher has both her guardian and her great aunt to look out for her wellbeing, perhaps you would have been wiser to consult them on the matter before taking it into you own hands. Has it not crossed your mind that as they are both clearly fond of Miss Fletcher, they might wish for such an alliance?"

"It is quite possible that you are correct, ma'am. But I know my charge better than anyone. It may be that she might develop a fondness for Mr Fancot – I have told him as much. But there will be no hope of it if he gives her a disgust for him by subjecting her to attentions that are, at present, unwanted."

She had made an effort to keep her tone even and reasonable, but she saw Mrs Fancot's eyes grow colder as she said the word disgust.

"If I might offer you some advice, Miss Hayes? Although you seem to be treated here as an equal, you would do well to remember that you are not, whatever your birth. And although I can fully understand that your uncertain future might encourage you to look for a husband, I suggest you look a little lower than the next Earl of Carstairs."

Sarah gasped, and her hands curled into fists.

"You might do worse than to follow my own example," she continued. "The vicar seems very much a gentleman, and is, I think, a much more realistic target in your present circumstances. I noticed that you had him hanging on your every word."

Sarah said in a tight voice, "I did not! And what is more, whilst I understand that every mother might think her son an eminently desirable catch, I can assure you that I have never had any such thoughts towards Mr Fancot or any other gentleman here."

Mrs Fancot raised a sceptical brow. "Yet I saw you riding with my son from my window, only the other morning. Alone. I am surprised you would set your charge such a poor example."

Sarah's eyes flashed. "I can assure you, ma'am, that our meeting was completely accidental."

Mrs Fancot seemed rather pleased by her loss of composure and said, with a small smile that did not reach her eyes, "If you say so, Miss Hayes."

Clearly feeling that she had made her point, she smiled at Charlotte and patted the empty place beside her on the sofa. "Please sit with me, Miss Fletcher. I would be very interested to hear how you found the waters at Weymouth."

Feeling quite perturbed by their conversation, Sarah stood and took a turn about the room. It was not incomprehensible that a mother's natural fondness for her son should have prompted such resentment at her words to him. It was also understandable that she might wish to promote her son's happiness and so his interest in Charlotte. But to accuse her of having an ulterior motive in warning him off, and going as far as to say it was for her own selfish ends, was completely uncalled for.

Finding no relief in the decorous steps she was forced to make about the room, she sat at the pianoforte and began to absentmindedly play a ditty.

"Move over, my dear."

She hit the wrong key and a discordant note jarred the air. She had not heard Lady Carstairs approach.

"You held your temper very well in check, I thought. Do not set any store by Mrs Fancot's words. She has lost her husband and now has only her son to focus her attentions on. I shudder to think how rude I might become if I lost Carstairs."

Sarah looked dismayed. "You heard? Do not tell me Charlotte did also."

Lady Carstairs shook her head. "No, I do not think it. On the occasions that I was forced to hold a dinner or attend a ball in India, for my husband's sake, I learned the art of holding a conversation even as I tuned in on another. There was much backstabbing and political manoeuvring there, and I found it a useful way to distinguish who was our friend or our enemy."

Sarah smiled. "You would make a formidable enemy, I think."

A wicked light entered her hostess's eyes. "I can think of one or two people who might agree with you. Now slide over," she said. "Let us set that tinder alight in a more productive way. You are, I assume, a proficient player?"

Sarah made room for her on the double seat. "I am, ma'am."

Lady Carstairs reached for a folder of music that lay on top of the instrument. She licked her finger and began to scan through the sheets.

"This one will do," she said. "It is a sonata by Bach in F major for four hands. Are you up to the challenge, Miss Hayes?"

Sarah's eyes lit up. "I am always up for a challenge, Lady Carstairs."

"Glad to hear it." She handed the score to her. "You had best peruse it for a few moments for it is quite intricate, not to mention quick in parts."

The door opened on her words, and the gentlemen entered the room.

"My lady," Lord Carstairs said reprovingly. "Can it be that you were going to give one of your rare performances without me being present? I protest, it is too bad of you! You know how much I enjoy listening to your playing."

Sarah was amused to see a faint flush of pleasure brighten Lady Carstairs' cheek. However, her voice was as astringent as usual as she said, "If you enjoy it so much, sir, you had best take a seat and let me get on with it!"

As the gentlemen moved to sit down, Charlotte came over to them. "Shall I turn the pages for you?"

"That would be very helpful, child," Lady Carstairs said. "We may go too fast for you to follow, so I shall nod when we reach the last few bars of each page."

Sarah placed the sheets on the stand and laid her long, slim fingers over the keys.

"Ready?" Lady Carstairs said.

"Ready," she confirmed.

They launched into the piece. Sarah was very accomplished on the instrument, but even so, a slight frown marred her brow as she concentrated on matching the lightness and speed of Lady Carstairs' fingers. They were well matched. Sarah relaxed as they attained a perfect unity in both pace and precision. The piece was both entertaining and uplifting, and as they reached the halfway point, they turned briefly to each other and exchanged a smile of mutual joy and appreciation.

As they finished with a flourish, the room erupted into applause.

"You outdid yourself, my dear," Lord Carstairs said, coming forwards. He took her hand and raised it to his lips.

"I needed to," she said. "I had stiff competition."

Lord Carstairs turned to Sarah and bowed. "My wife speaks the truth, Miss Hayes. Your play was also outstanding." His eyes turned to Charlotte. "And the page turner was without fault."

Charlotte laughed.

"Will you play something for us, my dear?"

She glanced a little nervously around the

room. "You cannot expect me to follow that performance, Uncle Oliver."

He looked a little disappointed, prompting Sarah to say gently, "You play quite well enough, Charlotte, and sing very sweetly. If you were to perhaps choose a folk song, the two performances would not be compared because they are both so very different."

"Splendid idea," said Sir Horace coming towards them. "Don't you worry, Miss Fletcher, I will turn the pages for you."

Lady Carstairs turned a surprised eye upon him. "You can read sheet music, sir?"

"Not a beat, ma'am. But I'm sure Miss Fletcher will tell me when to do the thing."

As Lady Carstairs drew a breath, Charlotte said quickly, "Thank you, sir. That is most obliging of you."

Sarah's amused eyes met Lord Seymore's and she saw her humour reflected there.

Charlotte flicked through the sheets of music until she came across a simple ballad that she recognised. She played it very creditably and, if her fingers occasionally stumbled over the keys when Sir Horace was a fraction too late in his office, her clear, pure voice made up for it.

"I say, Miss Fletcher," he said as she finished.

"I have rarely listened to anything I have enjoyed more."

She smiled up at him, only a little self-consciously, an imp of mischief in her eyes. "And do you often attend musical recitals, sir?"

"No," he admitted. "I was dragged to one such evening a few years ago…" he paused and grimaced. "It was excruciating."

"Then I can hardly take your words as a compliment, sir. You have little to compare it to, after all," she teased him gently.

"Well you're out there, Miss Fletcher. A man knows what he likes and what he don't, and that's all there is to it!"

The words were uttered with deep conviction, but in his usual abrupt manner, robbing them of any encroaching overtones, and so Charlotte found herself able to laugh.

When the tea tray was brought in, Mrs Fancot got to her feet. "I really must be going," she said softly. "Thank you for your kind hospitality, Lord and Lady Carstairs, but I am no longer used to company and feel quite overwhelmed."

Mr Fancot got immediately to his feet. "Of course, Mother. I will take you back."

Once they had left the room, Lady Carstairs said, "Sir Horace, sit with me, if you will. I hear you have travelled in Greece and Turkey. I would be very interested to hear your observations on these countries."

"Be happy to ma'am," he said cheerfully, sitting down beside her. "But don't hesitate to stop me if I rattle on a trifle."

"You may be sure that I won't," she said dryly.

However, she was surprised to discover that Sir Horace spoke like a sensible man on local customs, the many kindnesses he had received from the people, and the historical legacy of the places he had visited. By the time she rose to retire, she found she was more in charity with him than she would ever have expected to be.

CHAPTER 8

S arah came down early to take a ride before breakfast. As she requested Nyx to be made ready, Lord Seymore strode into the stables.

"Good day, Miss Hayes," he said smiling. "You are up with the lark. It seems we share a love of early mornings."

"Yes. I always used to ride before breakfast at home."

"Take your pick of the horses, sir. I'll be with you in a moment," Greeves said, walking over to the harness room.

"Leave it to me, Greeves," Lord Seymore said. "I believe I know how to saddle a horse."

He chose a fine looking stallion. Sarah watched with approval as he ran a confident hand over the horse before efficiently preparing him. By the time she was in the saddle, he was finished.

"I can see you've done that before, sir," Greeves said approvingly.

"Horses have always been my passion," he admitted. "I was forever getting under our groom's feet when I was a boy! I learned to do all the jobs in the stable."

Greeves raised a sceptical brow. "Even mucking out, sir?"

"Even mucking out," he grinned.

He glanced at Sarah. "Shall we ride together, Miss Hayes?"

Mrs Fancot's words of the evening before made her hesitate. Lord Seymore frowned.

"Of course, if you do not wish for my company, we will go our separate ways," he said coolly.

"No," she said quickly. "It is not that at all. How could you think I would be so surly?"

He raised an enquiring brow. "Well then, what is it?"

"It is nothing," she said. "I am merely refining too much on a few words that were said to me last evening."

She hoped he would leave it there. But once

they were clear of the yard, he asked her to explain.

She sighed. "Mrs Fancot saw her son riding with me the day you arrived. I had gone out alone and we met by chance, but she implied that my actions were not quite proper."

"Nonsense," he said. "You are in the country, after all, and as long as you stay within the grounds, I cannot see where the impropriety lays."

"No, that is what I thought," she said.

It occurred to her that she really ought to bring Mr Fancot's interest in his ward to Lord Seymore's attention. She had managed to snatch a few minutes with Lady Carstairs before they retired. Although she had admitted that it would give her great pleasure if Charlotte settled somewhere nearby, she had insisted that she would not encourage any match that might make the child unhappy.

"I am afraid I drew Mrs Fancot's displeasure down upon my head by giving Mr Fancot some advice, concerning Charlotte. I hope you do not think it was presumptuous of me."

"Why should, I?" he said bemused. "Charlotte is your concern. I saw the adroit way in which you extracted her from Mr Fancot's adoring clutches and was very grateful to you."

Her brows rose in surprise. "You realised?"

His eyes crinkled in a most attractive way when he smiled, she realised.

"You do have a very poor opinion of my powers of observation, Miss Hayes. I could hardly have failed to notice the way his eyes follow her around a room. The poor fellow has got a bad case of calf love, I think. He is, perhaps, a little old to be experiencing it, but then from what I can discover, he has been too taken up with overseeing things here to have had the opportunity to expand his horizons in other areas."

Sarah felt a quiver of indignation. A little effort on his part could have saved her from an awkward conversation and all the consequent unpleasantness that had followed. How very like him to have left it all to her.

"Did you not think to have a word in his ear?" she said, exasperated.

"I would certainly have done so if it had become necessary," he replied calmly. "But I could not see that Charlotte was in any danger. Mr Fancot does not seem the sort to foist unwelcome attentions on a defenceless female."

"That all depends on your definition of unwelcome attentions, sir. Charlotte is far more sensitive than your average young lady. Her friend, Miss Montagu, would most likely have questioned his choice of simile, or laughed outright at his flowery compliments, and Lady Georgianna would have turned him to stone with a look. But Charlotte is only made flustered, miserable, and a little afraid by such talk."

"You may be right, Miss Hayes," he said, unruffled by her heated assertions. "I could certainly see that she was made uncomfortable last evening, and I may have intervened if you had given me any opportunity to do so. But you, of all people, must realise that if she is to last five minutes in the company of some of the young bucks she will encounter in Town, then she must learn how to deal with comments that may be a little warmer than she could wish. She will not always have you there by her side, after all."

Sarah opened her mouth to speak but then shut it again. In all fairness, she could not deny that his words held some truth. She had rushed into precipitate action the moment she had seen Charlotte was distressed, in the same way she had if a girl at school had made a spiteful comment to her. Her instinct had always been to shield her from adversity.

"I may have been a little overprotective of her," she acknowledged with some difficulty. "But when I arrived at the seminary, she had hidden away in a dark place deep inside herself. I coaxed her from that place, inch by slow inch, and I would fight tooth and nail to keep her from retreating to such a place again."

"I know," he said gently. "But I do not think she is any danger of it, do you?"

"Not at present," she agreed. "She is much improved since she has come here. But although her confidence is growing, it is still a fragile thing."

"Then we must strengthen it, ma'am. You must lead by example. You have only to be yourself, after all."

"Oh?" she said, mistrusting the lurking twinkle in his eyes.

"Indeed. She has only seen the modest, patient teacher. Show her some of your other attributes."

"Which ones did you have in mind?" she said, raising an arch brow.

He looked reflective. "Let me see. Spirit, boldness, a managing disposition, prickliness, but not," he assured her, "surliness."

A reluctant grin twitched her lips. "Impossible man!"

"I do not admit to it. Come," he said moving into a canter, "let us blow away these crochets."

The morning air was fresh, dew sparkled on

the grass they raced over, and the dawn chorus welcomed in the day with optimistic cheer. She felt her spirits lift. Lord Seymore was an excellent horseman and he matched her stride for stride. Her breath caught in her throat as he suddenly turned to her, a reckless grin stretching across his face and an excited gleam, so like her father's, shining in his deep, blue eyes.

"Whoever is last to the stand of trees ahead, may ask the other two questions which they must answer truthfully. Do you accept this wager?"

He had checked his horse slightly as he spoke. She wrinkled her brow as if she were considering this unusual request, but then urged Nyx to pick up her speed, throwing her agreement over her shoulder as she raced ahead.

The trees were only a few hundred yards away, and she kept her eyes firmly fixed on her goal as she heard his mount's hooves thundering behind her. A triumphant smile widened her lips as she covered the last twenty yards, but when she was but a few strides away, he passed her. They allowed their mounts to slow gradually, and then turned them towards the river.

"You do not play fair, ma'am," he protested, but with a smile.

"Perhaps not," she agreed. "But you have

the more powerful horse, sir, and so I felt it only fair to give myself a small advantage."

"And you do not like to lose, I think," he grinned.

"No more than you, I suspect," she said. "A true gentleman might have let a lady claim the victory."

"Would that have given you any satisfaction, Miss Hayes?"

She laughed. "No. It would not."

They had come to the river. As she approached the bridge, she saw someone sat upon his coat on the riverbank, rapidly sketching. She was most surprised when he turned his head and she perceived it was Sir Horace. The reason for this astonishment was not only his occupation and the frown that momentarily marred his usually genial countenance, but also his attire. Gone were all the adjuncts of the dandy. He wore a comfortable pair of buckskins, a smart but unassuming beige waistcoat, and his shirt sleeves were rolled up to his elbows. As he stood and offered her a bow, she saw a pair of serviceable top boots had replaced his gleaming hessians.

"I did not recognise you, sir," she said, smiling.

"Oh, I never wear town garb when I'm in the country. Not in the day, at least. Only thing was, I didn't have anything else with me. I sent to Netherhampton for my country togs almost as soon as I arrived. It's only a day away, you know."

"What on earth has brought you out at such an hour, Bamber?" Lord Seymore enquired.

"Birds," he said. "I hoped to spot a king-fisher; they're dashed elusive creatures and are often most active first thing in the morning."

"And did you, sir?" Sarah enquired.

"Yes, two of them. But I'm afraid you've frightened them off."

He turned the sketchpad in his hand and her brows rose. He had completed a series of sketches, some of them capturing the bird in flight. The central drawing, depicted the little bird sat upon a branch, and although not quite finished, it was quite exquisite. He had used pastels to capture the iridescent turquoise of its wings and bright orange breast.

"It is beautiful, Sir Horace. Do show Miss Fletcher, she used to amuse herself seeing how many different birds she could see in the grounds at the seminary."

"Did she, by Jove?" he said, brightening. "Then I shall most certainly show her. I'll see you both at breakfast, must just finish this."

Sarah went first across the bridge, suddenly

feeling a little uneasy as she pondered what Lord Seymore might ask her. He must have seen as much in her expression, for when they reached the path through the wood and he drew alongside her, he gently shook his head.

"I will claim my prize another time, Miss Hayes. We seem to have reached some sort of understanding today, and I would not jeopardise it so soon. But make no mistake, I shall ask those questions."

"Of course. I never renege on a wager." She threw a glance towards the dower house and gave a low chuckle. "If Mrs Fancot could hear me she would add gambling to all my other faults."

"I expect, having lived for many years as a vicar's wife in a small parish, she might easily be shocked. If I told her, for example, that you raced two gentlemen one morning in Hyde Park, you would be quite sunk beneath reproach."

"You wouldn't!" Sarah gasped. "Besides, it was very early, hardly any one was about, and one of them was my father."

"True. Who was the other gentleman, I forget."

"Mr Aldersney."

Lord Seymore frowned. "Aldersney? Oh yes,

I have it. He was that odd chap who was horse mad and always wore his riding gear, whatever the occasion."

"That's it," Sarah said, laughing. "He was very eccentric. He met us exercising our horses and was foolish enough to say that I rode quite well – for a female."

"Ah, I see. I suppose it was inevitable you would challenge him to a race."

"Not at all," she said primly, the effect ruined by the sparkle in her eyes. "I would not have dreamed of doing such a shocking thing."

Lord Seymore raised sceptical brows.

"It is true. I was not so brazen. It was my father who took exception. He told him in no uncertain terms that I could ride as well as any of the gentlemen about Town, and better than most."

He smiled. "He was right."

"Thank you. Mr Aldersney, however, would not believe it. It was then my father suggested the race."

"And you beat him hollow."

"Oh no. It was a very close run thing. I won only by a head, Mr Aldersney was second, and my father was only half a head behind him."

Lord Seymore grinned. "I wish I had witnessed it. He must have been most put out."

"Not at all. He asked my father for his permission to marry me, there and then. He said he wouldn't have believed it if he hadn't seen it with his own eyes, and he was never likely to find another filly who would suit him half so well."

Their laughter was interrupted by raised voices coming from the direction of the dower house. They exchanged a look and then turned their horses onto the smaller track that led there. As they came into the clearing, they saw that it was a very attractive building. Beneath its thatched roof, latticed windows twinkled in the sunlight, and rambling roses climbed the walls and framed the front door.

The raised voices ceased and the door was suddenly thrown open, none too gently. Mr Fancot strode out of the house in such a hurry that he did not even pause to close it behind him. He seemed to be in quite a pelter, for he offered them no more than a nod before continuing past them and disappearing into the wood. His mother appeared in the doorway. She had a handkerchief clutched in one hand, and upon seeing them she raised it to her eyes and hastily dabbed at them.

Sarah swiftly dismounted in her unique manner, and hurried towards her.

"Mrs Fancot, I am sorry to see you so distressed." She laid a hand on her arm as she spoke. "Please, let me take you back inside."

Mrs Fancot shook her head and stepped away from her. "Thank you, but I will be quite alright now," she said in faint accents. She raised large eyes that were swimming in tears. "He has such a temper. His father was just the same. But do not concern yourself, Miss Hayes. A good walk usually sets him to rights."

She stepped back inside the house and closed the door. Sarah stared at it in blank astonishment for a moment. Although she had seen the occasional flash of irritation in Mr Fancot's eyes, she would never have suspected him of having such an unruly temper that he would raise his voice to his mother.

She turned and discovered that Lord Seymore had dismounted and was waiting by Nyx.

"Shall I help you?" he said, with a lopsided grin. "Or have you also developed an interesting way to get *into* the saddle?"

She smiled, but it was a little half-hearted. The strange spectacle they had witnessed had dampened her good humour a little.

"I have," she admitted. "But as it is extremely unladylike, I will accept your aid, sir."

"You seem quite perturbed, Miss Hayes," he said as they rode towards the house.

"I am a little surprised," she admitted. "I had thought Mr Fancot to be a quite devoted son."

"Perhaps he has been a little too devoted," he said. "He has been cooped up in that house with his mother for the best part of a year. And did I not hear the vicar say she was something of a recluse?"

"Yes, he did say that," she said thoughtfully.

"I am not at all sure it is healthy for a young man of such energy to have clipped his wings for so long."

"No, I agree. He had the run of the hall to himself before he brought his mother here. I can quite understand that to be suddenly restricted and watched over so closely might rub him up the wrong way occasionally."

After breakfast they all walked into the village for the Sunday morning service. Sarah was not surprised that the church was well attended, for Mr Bamber certainly had presence. He spoke long and eloquently on the theme of forbearance and when he uttered the words: *If you receive offence, be instantly ready to forgive on the first acknowledgment of the fault, even as Christ forgave you,* she could not help glancing in Mr Fancot's direction. His face remained as stony and cold as the finely carved pillar that rose behind him, however.

She had thought that the vicar's choice of sermon was extremely apposite after this morning's events, and could almost credit him with a startling degree of prescience. However, his true motive soon became apparent. As he shook his brother's hand on his way out of the church, he lay his other on his shoulder and gave him a wry smile.

"I hope you will forgive me, Horace, when I own that I have used you shamefully."

Sir Horace was not prone to reflect on unpleasant memories, and had a very real affection for his brother. He beamed at him, and shook his hand vigorously.

"There is nothing to forgive, my dear Loftus. I am very happily circumstanced as it happens and it is all thanks to you. If you hadn't had that dashed queer turn, I might never have been invited up to the hall, and that you know, would have been a great deal too bad."

The vicar did not so much as blink at this reference to his health. "I am humbled by your generosity of spirit, Horace. I hope it will not be lessened by any noticeable degree when I inform you that I am expecting a visit from our esteemed mother in the near future."

"No, why should it?" he said. His face suddenly fell. "That is, unless... dash it all, Loftus, do not tell me she is bringing that gal, Jane, or Anne, or some such thing, with her?"

A strange noise somewhere between a squeak and a most unladylike snort escaped Sarah. Her eyes met Lord Seymore's for a moment, and she saw her amusement reflected there. He offered her his handkerchief and she thankfully blew her nose.

"No, Horace. I will not tell you that. It appears that mother was less than pleased with Jane, and has sent her home."

Sir Horace's brow cleared. "Well, that's all right and tight then. I must say, Loftus, you get some very odd ideas in that cockloft of yours. Why would I mind mother paying a visit? I'm very fond of her. I tell you what it is; I think you are working too hard."

"God's work is never a chore, Horace," he said, a little reprovingly.

"No, no, of course not, old fellow. I didn't mean to imply, that is—"

"I know what the thing is, never fear," he said relenting.

Sir Horace looked relieved and moved on to make way for the next person in the long line of people who wished for a word with his brother.

The party had just reached the churchyard gate, when a high-pitched, rather piercing voice issued from behind them.

"Cooee, Lady Carstairs. Oh, Lady Carstairs!"

Sarah thought she heard Lady Carstairs utter a quite shocking expletive beneath her breath. However, when she turned she had pinned a smile upon her lips.

A rather plump lady of middling years was running down the path, clutching her hat to her head with one hand. She came to a stop before them, and gasped, "I am so glad I caught you, Lady Carstairs. I was quite hoping that you would return the visit I paid you a sennight past, but now I see that you have guests, I shall forgive you the oversight."

"How very kind of you, Lady Truboot," she said, without any real conviction.

When she did not offer any further encouragement, her lord stepped in and introduced their visitors.

"What a merry party you must be," she trilled. "That brings me to what I wished to say to you, Lady Carstairs. We are giving a little dinner on Friday, and I would be delighted if you, Lord Carstairs, Mr Fancot, oh, and indeed all your party would come."

Lady Carstairs' smile widened. "How very kind of you, Lady Truboot. We would all be delighted, I am sure, but unfortunately we are attending the assembly rooms in Weymouth on Friday."

A determined and rather hard gleam entered Lady Truboot's eyes. "Did I say Friday? Oh, how foolish of me. I had meant to say Wednesday."

She turned to her husband, a rather faded looking man about Lord Carstairs' age, as he came up to her with a young lady on his arm. "Sir Richard, please add your voice to mine. Would it not be splendid if Lady Carstairs brought her party to our dinner on Wednesday?"

She placed a slight emphasis on the last word. He clearly knew his duty, for once he had removed his hat, bowed, and introduced his daughter, Miss Emma Truboot, he said gently, "Yes, please do come."

His eyes rested on Charlotte for a moment. "It would be so very pleasant for Emma to have another lady her age visit, for there is only Amelia Shadstow who lives in the neighbourhood, but she has gone with her mother to Bath. I fear my Emma has been rather lonely of late."

Miss Truboot blushed at the attention this

drew to herself. She had been staring rather fixedly at the floor, but now looked up, revealing a face that whilst not beautiful, was made pretty by a pair of intelligent eyes and the soft bloom of youth that shone in her smooth pink cheeks.

Lady Carstairs regarded her husband and some unspoken message seemed to pass between them. She turned back to Lady Truboot and said, "How fortunate you realised your mistake, ma'am. We are indeed free on Wednesday and would be delighted to attend your dinner."

That Mr Bamber's powerful sermon had not overly impressed Mr Fancot, was borne out when he did not rush back to the dower house to make his peace with his parent. It became clear at dinner that evening that any hope of a swift rapprochement seemed increasingly unlikely. After the first course had been removed, Lord Carstairs tapped his fork lightly against his wine glass. The resonating ring hung in the air for a few seconds, drawing everyone's attention.

"I am happy to inform you, that as from this evening, Mr Charles Fancot will be taking up his old rooms in the east wing."

He glanced around the table at the various surprised expressions of the other diners and added gently, "It is only right that as my heir, he should do so."

"Of course it is," confirmed Lady Carstairs. "But what about Mrs Fancot, Carstairs? I think that perhaps we should encourage her to also come. We have room enough, after all."

"No!" Mr Fancot coloured as all eyes swivelled in his direction. "My mother would not accept such an invitation," he said in gentler tones. "She finds it difficult to be around people, especially strangers. She was quite exhausted after her last visit."

"Of course she does," Lord Carstairs said soothingly. He looked towards his lady, a warm expression in his eyes. "Your kind consideration is to be admired, my dear. I have always thought you are a most superior woman."

A pleased smile crossed her face but she said, "Don't try to flummery me, Carstairs. You would think any female who agreed with you a superior female!"

"Although it pains me to disagree with you, my dear, I must tell you that you are mistaken. But do not worry about Mrs Fancot, I will take it upon myself to pay a brief visit to that good lady once a day until she has become accustomed to the absence of her son."

Her smile faded. "You need not trouble yourself, Carstairs. That task should fall to me."

"No, my lady," he said in soft, but implacable tones. "You already have your hands full. Besides, between you and Charles, I am left with very little to do. Let me perform this one small task, will you?"

Lady Carstairs' eyes dropped from his. "As you wish."

CHAPTER 9

Sir Horace had enjoyed a reprieve from the daunting task of improving his dancing, as it was not considered appropriate to partake in such a frivolous activity on a Sunday. But the following morning, after breakfast, Sarah and Charlotte came upon him crossing the hall in the direction of the front door.

"Sir Horace," Sarah said. "Have you forgotten our appointment in the drawing room?"

He coloured slightly and stammered, "N-no, n-no, of course not. But on second thoughts, I think it would be better if we started with the riding lessons."

Charlotte exchanged an amused glance with her companion. "But I am not dressed for riding, and I see you have your sketch pad with you, sir. Did you intend to draw the horse as well?"

His eyes met hers for a pregnant moment and then he smiled bashfully. "Been caught red-handed, haven't I?"

"Yes," she laughed. "There really is no need for you to sneak off, you know. I will not think any less of you just because you might stand on my toes."

"There's no might about it," he said ruefully. "Bound to. Have never managed to get through a dance without standing on someone's toes."

Charlotte took his arm and began walking with him towards the drawing room. "You really only need master a few basic steps, you know. The trick is to perform them in a neat and timely manner."

"I will do my best, ma'am," he assured her.

"You can do no more," she said.

Sarah smiled at this flow of gentle encouragement. It was given in a style that she herself had often adopted with Charlotte when she was uncertain of something.

"I suggest we start with a country dance," she said, going over to the pianoforte and picking up the folder of music. "It is not ideal that there are only two of you, but we will lay out some chairs to represent the other people in the set. You will just have to use a little bit of imagination."

A faint sheen of perspiration dampened Sir Horace's frowning brow as he concentrated fiercely on his steps. But when he crushed Charlotte's slipper beneath his boot for the second time, he dropped her hand abruptly and exclaimed in frustration, "You see, it is no good. I am a hopeless case."

"Nonsense, Sir Horace. You must not give up now. I did not think you such a poor creature."

Sarah hid a smile at her ward's censorious words.

"It is not that I wish to renege on our bargain, Miss Fletcher. I am a man of my word, I assure you. But I am afraid that I will do you a serious injury, and then you will be unable to dance with anyone at the ball."

"That would not concern me overly, I assure you."

He gave her a stern look. "Now who is the poor creature? It will not do. You shall dance at the ball. Most people thoroughly enjoy it and I would not wish you to miss out on anything that might give you pleasure. It is only clumsy oafs like me to whom it is torture."

"You are not clumsy or an oaf," Charlotte

reprimanded him. "I will not hear you put yourself down so."

"Not putting myself down," he protested. "Just stating the facts, ma'am."

"The fault does not lay with you, sir."

Sir Horace looked bemused. "Well, as these wayward feet belong to me, I don't see who else's fault it can be."

"The fault lies with whoever taught you to dance."

Sir Horace did not look convinced. "It does, eh?"

"It most definitely does. They certainly do not deserve the title of dancing master, for I am no expert, yet I have already realised where the problem lies," she assured him.

A gleam of hope brightened Sir Horace's eyes. "You have?"

"Yes. You have the steps, Sir Horace, but if you don't mind me saying so, your timing is not all it should be."

"So that's it, is it?"

"Indeed it is. I believe that you are concentrating so hard on your steps that you are quite forgetting to listen to the music. Even your bow at the very beginning was a little late. We shall start again, and I do not want you to so much as glance at your feet; they already know what to do. I wish you to do nothing but listen to the music and watch when I curtsey. Then we will practice that part together."

Charlotte nodded at Sarah and she launched into the introduction. Sir Horace cocked his head to one side as he listened, and noted carefully when Charlotte took a small step to the side, curtsied, and stepped back into her original position.

"Now we will do it together. Ready?"

"Yes, I think I've got it," he said.

It seemed that he had, for they moved together in perfect unison.

"Bravo," Sarah said. "That was much better, Sir Horace."

Charlotte bade him listen and watch her again. This time, after she had made her curtsey and stepped back into position, she gave her hand to an imaginary partner and skipped around the first chair and returned. When Sir Horace completed this manoeuvre with her in a neat and timely manner, a wide grin crossed his face.

"Miss Fletcher, you are a miracle worker."

When he managed to repeat the performance, and skip in a circle holding Charlotte's hands without once stepping on her toes, Sarah was inclined to agree with him. But as she had always believed you should quit whilst winning, she got up from the pianoforte after this seemingly impossible feat had been achieved.

Sir Horace looked a little crestfallen. "We are not stopping already, surely? We have only just begun."

"And it is a very promising beginning, sir," she said, smiling. "But I have always believed that it is better to work on a skill little and often. We shall practise again this afternoon."

He accepted this pronouncement with good grace. "I never thought I would say these words, but I shall look forward to it. I am really very grateful to you both. Now, Miss Fletcher, I shall carry out my part in this bargain. Whilst you get changed, I shall see your horse is made ready."

"Oh, yes, of course," she said, a little doubtfully.

"Come now, Miss Fletcher," Sir Horace said in rallying tones. "There is no need to feel any anxiety. You will be quite safe, I assure you."

"I will come up and help you change," Sarah said, taking her by the arm.

She had given her one of her own habits, and Charlotte had made the necessary adjustments the previous day. Made of fine Merino cloth in Florentia blue, it suited her colouring and almost perfectly matched the blue of her eyes. Set atop her blonde locks was a military cap of the same colour, ornamented with feathers dyed to match.

"You look very well," Sarah said. "That colour suits you far more than it did me."

"Thank you." Charlotte swiftly kissed her cheek. "You are so good to me. This habit and the ball gown you have gifted me are by far the most beautiful items in my wardrobe."

Sarah gently pinched her cheek. "Do not be such a goose. I have far more finery than I need. Once you go to London, Lady Carstairs will deck you out in fine style, I am sure, but in the meantime it is my pleasure to donate the odd item from my wardrobe. I will have little use for half of my things when I go back to the seminary, after all."

Charlotte frowned a little at this, but only said, "Will you come down with me?"

"Not this time," Sarah said. "I would not wish Sir Horace to feel that I did not trust him, besides, the vicar has assured me that his brother is quite able to teach you."

But when Charlotte left the room, Sarah counted to twenty and then hastily followed. She swiftly crossed the great hall and disappeared into the east wing. She passed the drawing room and library, and made her way to a side door. Beyond it, a short stretch of grass brought her to the back of the stable buildings. She followed the wall of the coach house to its end, and then peeped cautiously around the corner of the building. Seeing that Charlotte and Sir Horace were waiting outside the stalls with their backs to her, she came around the corner and nipped inside the coach house.

She leaned back against the wall for a moment and gave a low laugh. It was quite ridiculous for her to be sneaking about in this furtive manner. She was determined not to be quite so protective of Charlotte, which was why she had resisted the temptation to accompany her when given the choice. She would just satisfy herself that Sir Horace was up to the job, and then she would leave them to it.

She gave a gasp of dismay as a long shadow, unmistakably that of a man, suddenly darkened the floor. A moment later, Lord Seymore strode into the coach house, his dark brows slashing downwards in a frown. He glanced quickly about the room and then turned his head and spotted her.

Sarah sighed. "You have found me out, sir," she said quietly.

"So it would appear," he said dryly, his expression lightening. "Whatever are you doing, Miss Hayes?"

She hastily put her finger to her lips. "Shh! I do not wish Charlotte or Sir Horace to know that I am here."

He looked back over his shoulder and saw a horse being led out into the yard.

"Ah, so that is it."

Sarah felt a blush stain her cheeks. "Yes. I did not wish to be in the way."

"Clearly," he said. "I take it you do not trust Sir Horace in this matter. You can, you know."

"I am sure you are right, sir. But I would like to see for myself. Now, please, come away from the doorway or they will see you."

When he moved a little to one side, Sarah turned, and peeped out. She saw Charlotte put her foot into Sir Horace's hands, and then her hand on his shoulder before reaching for the saddle. Each movement was done slowly and deliberately as if she were carefully following instructions. But before she could mount, the horse sidled a little. She let go of the saddle and stepped away from Sir Horace.

"The horse can probably sense her fear," Lord Seymore said softly.

Sarah nodded. Sir Horace's voice, unusually sharp, cut across the yard.

"Hold her still will you?"

The stable boy took a firmer hold on the bridle, but Greeves appeared and sent him away with a flea in his ear. He positioned himself at the mare's head.

Sir Horace bent and again offered his hands, but straightened when Charlotte shook her head.

"It might have been useful if you had shown her how it is done," Lord Seymore said conversationally.

"I am trying to make her more independent," Sarah hissed, straightening. "But I shall go and offer my help."

"Do not be so hasty, Miss Hayes. Look."

Sarah poked her head around the door once more. Charlotte was now standing with her back to the horse. As they watched, Sir Horace grasped her waist firmly, and lifted her into the saddle. Once safely delivered there, he mimed as well as spoke his directions. They saw him lift his own leg and move it to the side. Charlotte followed suit and lifted her leg over the pommel. He then turned his hips a little and straightened his back. Charlotte adjusted her posture slightly. Seemingly satisfied, he then took the reins from Greeves and began slowly walking the horse around the yard.

As he turned it in their direction, they both quickly stepped back from the doorway. Their eyes met and they both smiled.

"Satisfied, Miss Hayes?"

"Yes. He will do very well."

Sarah had expected Sir Horace would take Charlotte into the park, but after a few minutes, it became clear he was not so ambitious.

"As it appears we are stuck here for the time being, what say we take a look at the carriages?" Lord Seymore suggested.

Apart from his own curricle and the barouche, which Sarah had already seen, there was a coach bearing the eagle crest, another curricle, and hidden away in a dark corner, a lightly sprung high-perch phaeton.

Sarah's eyes lit up.

"Yes, this is more your style, I think," Lord Seymore said, smiling. "Although it as not as smart as yours was."

"You remember?" Sarah said, surprised.

"Yes, but it is the lovely pair of matching grays that pulled it, which really caught my attention."

She laughed. "Your own chestnuts are just as fine, I think. I do believe you are as horse mad as Mr Aldersney."

"Perhaps," he acknowledged. "But at least I do not turn up to dinner in my riding garb."

Their smiling eyes met and locked. She had seen eyes of such a deep blue only once before. They had belonged to Charlotte's fellow pupil, Lady Georgianna Voss. But whereas hers were cool and distant, Lord Seymore's were warmed by amusement, and she somehow found herself quite mesmerised by them.

"Oh dear. I hope I have not stumbled upon a secret assignation."

Sarah started and turned swiftly. "Lord Carstairs. It is no such thing."

He smiled gently at her. "Of course it is not. I was only teasing you, Miss Hayes. I have just come back from visiting Mrs Fancot and heard voices. As most of the stable hands seem unaccountable interested in Charlotte being led in circles around the yard, I did wonder who might be in here. I see you are admiring the phaeton."

"Yes," she said. "It looks to be very nicely balanced."

Seeing the look of mild surprise that crossed his host's face, Lord Seymore said, "Miss Hayes used to tool a high-perch phaeton around the park in Town, sir, pulled by two of the finest horses I have ever seen."

"How splendid," he said. "I do so hate

167

seeing things go to waste, so you must feel free to take it out, Miss Hayes."

"Oh," she breathed. "I couldn't poss—"

"Nonsense," he interrupted. "It has been stood gathering dust for far too long. Things left too long inactive, tend to wither and die. Lord Seymore can go with you if you are worried."

She looked up and saw him raise a questioning brow.

"Would you like to come, sir?"

"Yes," he said firmly. "I would."

"Good, very good," said Lord Carstairs. "You will have to wait until tomorrow, however. A few of the other vehicles will need to be moved, and the phaeton needs a thorough clean."

He suddenly frowned, his eyes lost focus as if he were thinking of something, and he put one hand to his chest and rubbed it a little.

"Are you alright, sir?" Sarah said, concerned.

"Yes, I am quite alright now," he said. "Just a bit of my old trouble."

"Your old trouble?"

"It is nothing," he assured her. "I occasionally suffer from palpitations, usually when I have overexerted myself. I shall go and lie down for a while. That usually puts things to rights."

"Would you like to take my arm, sir?" Sarah said gently.

"No," he smiled. "It is very kind of you, my dear, but I do not wish to draw any undue attention to myself."

Lord Seymore looked at him closely. There was a faint sheen of perspiration on his brow. "Shall I fetch the doctor?"

"No, I thank you. Augusta already worries enough. I would ask you not to mention this to her. It will pass. It always does."

Sarah could not feel quite comfortable with his request. He seemed to sense it, for he took her hand in his own and patted it.

"I promise you, Miss Hayes, that if it does not pass, or begins to occur more than usual, I will inform Augusta and send for the doctor. Does that satisfy you?"

"Yes, I suppose so," she said reluctantly.

CHAPTER 10

They agreed to take the phaeton out before breakfast in lieu of their morning ride. Lord Seymore arrived first and strode up and down the yard as he waited for her. He was, he realised, looking forward to their drive. When she forgot to be angry with him, Miss Hayes was really very good company.

A wry smile twisted his lips as he recalled how often he had wished that it had been he, and not Lord Turnbull, who sat beside Miss Hayes as she drove her grays around the park. If wishes had been arrows, Turnbull would have been pierced through the heart many times. Having benefited from a few seasons in Town, that gentleman had all the polish that he had sorely lacked. His commonplace compliments and adoring stares had not been a match for Turnbull's wit and charm. It was just as well; he had been far too young to form a lasting attachment to anyone. In all truth, his heart burnings had been more posture than anything else. It had been far more comfortable to admire Miss Hayes from afar.

He, and a few of his cronies, had almost felt obliged to pay homage to the latest incomparable, and had spent many an enjoyable evening drowning their sorrows when they had seen the way the wind was blowing.

He came to a halt in front of the coach house as the phaeton was led out, and shook his head as he remembered the foolish thought that had briefly gripped him the day before. He had come out of the library just in time to see Miss Hayes hurriedly disappearing through the side door. Both her haste and furtive manner had intrigued him and so he had followed her. When he had heard her low laugh issuing from the coach house, he had been both surprised and dismayed. The unwelcome thought that she might have crept out to meet someone had crossed his mind. Lord Carstairs, he knew, was visiting Mrs Fancot, and as he had just left an unaccountably out of sorts Lady Carstairs in the library, and both Sir Horace and Charlotte were in plain sight, that left only Mr Fancot.

Although he knew it to be unreasonable of him, for the briefest moment he had wondered if, in rescuing Charlotte from that gentleman's attentions, she was also serving her own interests. He had dismissed the thought almost immediately; she showed him no particular partiality. As soon as his eyes had alighted on her, he had felt relieved that his ward's companion would not behave in so reprehensible a manner. When he had ascertained her true reason for being there, he had also felt a little ashamed. Charlotte was always her first concern.

He grinned. How angry she would have been if she could have divined his thoughts. She was no longer the fearless, bold creature he remembered, but nor was she the modest mannered teacher he was sure she had tried very hard to become. The way her eyes had flashed at him in annoyance when he had suggested that it might have been better if she had demonstrated to Charlotte how to mount her horse, proved it.

"Good morning, Lord Seymore. A penny for your thoughts; you look very amused by something."

"Good morning, Miss Hayes," he said, bowing. "I was just daydreaming, I assure you."

For a moment he thought she was going to press him further, but then her glance strayed past his shoulder and her eyes widened.

"You are going to let me drive your chestnuts? How very kind of you."

"It is not really," he said. "I am merely ensuring my own comfort, ma'am. I could not find a pair that quite matched in Lord Carstairs' stables. Besides, I would not do so if I did not know you are a fine whip."

"As to that, sir," she said, "I feel it only right to warn you that I am bound to be a little rusty."

"If I feel either myself or my horses to be in any danger, you may be sure I shall take the reins from you."

Her brows rose. "I do not think that will be necessary, sir."

He hid a smile as he handed her up into the phaeton. How easily she rose to the fly. The urge to tease her was almost irresistible.

Barely had he taken his seat beside her, when she gracefully flicked the whip and set the horses to a brisk trot. A stable boy, who was lackadaisically sweeping the cobbles, jumped back hastily as Greeves gave a warning shout. She kept up a spanking pace all the way down the drive, only slowing as they approached the main gate.

"I wonder if I should have brought a horn?" Lord Seymore said pensively.

"To alert the toll-gate keeper? As we are in no hurry, sir, I hardly think it necessary."

"Oh, I quite agree," he said pleasantly. "I was rather thinking it would come in useful to clear the road, so you don't leave a trail of bodies behind you."

She smiled. "You mean the stable boy, I suppose. It was quite his own fault and anyway, a small fright will do him good. Next time he will pay more attention."

"You are severe, ma'am."

"Perhaps. But vehicles and riders come and go all the time in a stable yard, and the stable hands need to stay alert or there could be a nasty accident. I really think Greeves needs to be a little firmer with his boys. If my father had caught them all standing around gawping as they did yesterday when Charlotte was being led around the yard, he would have had something to say, you may be certain."

"I assume he ran a tight ship?" Lord Seymore said gently.

Sarah raised an eyebrow. "Of course he did…"

She broke off and her hands slackened on the reins for a moment. "At least, he did where his horses were concerned."

He heard sadness and regret in her voice, but he resisted the urge to offer her sympathy, somehow knowing that it would be unwelcome.

"I think you will find, Miss Hayes, that their inattention to their duties is not habitual. Charlotte presented a very pretty picture in her habit. I had never seen her look quite so fetching. I assume I have you to thank for that?"

"She did, didn't she?" she agreed, a note of pride in her voice. "But please do not thank me for giving her one of my castoffs. I never really liked the colour on me."

His eyes rested for a moment on her rather severe slate grey riding habit and matching round hat of moss silk. Not every lady could have carried it off, but it suited Miss Hayes' slim figure, and emphasised the bright lustre of her hair and eyes.

"Which way?" she asked.

"Through the village," he replied.

She entered Priddleton at a sedate trot and pulled up when she saw the vicar standing by the church gate, watching their progress.

"Good morning, Mr Bamber," she said, smiling. "I am pleased to report that your brother's dancing lessons are progressing very nicely."

Lord Seymore frowned a little as he saw a glimmer of appreciation brighten the vicar's eyes as they rested – a little too long in his opinion – on Miss Hayes.

"I am pleased to hear it, ma'am. But if you expect me to be surprised, I fear you will be disappointed. You appear to be a very accomplished lady. You certainly handle the ribbons in excellent form. Is there anything that you cannot turn your hand to?"

Lord Seymore raised a brow and glanced at Miss Hayes, interested at how she would take this flattery. He was pleased that she laughed it off.

"The credit for Sir Horace's improvement must go to Miss Fletcher. I have had very little to do with it. And there are a host of things I do not excel at, I assure you."

Mr Bamber looked sceptical. "Your modesty becomes you, ma'am. But I think if that really is the case, it must be due to a lack of interest in those things rather than any inherent lack of ability."

"Good morning, Vicar," Lord Seymore said, tipping his hat, "we must be on our way or we shall be late for breakfast."

Miss Hayes made no objection and he soon directed her down a lane to their left.

"I admit that I am intrigued. What are these things you do not excel at?"

"My mastery of the harp is rudimentary, and my Italian only passable," she informed him promptly.

He laughed. "You relieve my mind, Miss Hayes. I would not like to think that Charlotte's education had been lacking in any of the necessary accomplishments."

"You need have no fear," she assured him. "Have you forgotten that you paid the extra sum required to acquire for her the services of an excellent Italian tutor?"

When he informed her that of course he had not, she threw him a sceptical glance, leaving him in no doubt that although she now regarded him with a friendlier eye, he was far from being first oars with her. He was surprised to find this rankled a little. What a conceited fellow he was becoming. However much he enjoyed her company, the fact remained that she was not comfortable wife material, and so he had no right to wish that she would bestow any marked degree of approval upon him.

They returned to the house by a different

route. Sarah slowed the horses and came to a halt beside a gateway.

"So this is where you access the dower house from the road," she said.

A short gravelled driveway led to the back of the house. It bordered a very pleasant garden. Part of it was laid to lawn, but a substantial amount was given over to growing flowers, herbs, and vegetables. The different areas were divided into neat compartments by low hedges.

Mrs Fancot, it seemed, shared Lady Carstairs' love of gardening, for she was leaning over one of the hedges, clipping a few leaves from it. She suddenly looked up, but before they could call a greeting, she picked up a basket that lay at her feet and hurried into the house.

"Poor lady," Sarah said. "I should have been more considerate towards her on our first meeting. She must be so lonely without her husband, and now her son, to keep her company. If she would only go to church, she might feel less isolated and gradually begin to feel less overwhelmed by the presence of other people."

"Grief is a strange bedfellow," Lord Seymore said reflectively. "My own father became very withdrawn for a time after my mother died."

"Yes, it is," Sarah murmured, encouraging the horses into a trot.

"Do you still miss your father very much?" Lord Seymore asked gently.

"I often think of him," Sarah acknowledged. "Especially when I am riding."

She turned towards him and for once her expression was unguarded. Her eyes held a softness and vulnerability he had not seen before.

"You are the first person I have been able to talk to about him. Perhaps it is because you knew me before he…when he was still alive. When we laughed about that ridiculous race the other morning, I realised how far I had come. To be able to share a pleasant memory meant a great deal to me. Thank you."

He resisted the urge to touch her gloved hand, for her colour was heightened as if she were embarrassed by the admission.

"I am glad," he said simply. "I missed my own father terribly at first. He was a cantankerous old boot, but I was very fond of him."

Sarah smiled. "No wonder you deal so well with Lady Carstairs!"

He laughed. "Yes, he was very much in the same style, although she has not been on quite such good form of late. She seemed very subdued yesterday. Do you think she suspects that Lord Carstairs is not well?"

"I do not think that is it," she said thoughtfully. "If I am not much mistaken she is a little unhappy that he is going to visit Mrs Fancot."

"Surely you *are* mistaken, Miss Hayes. It was Lady Carstairs who was concerned that she was alone and suggested that she came to stay at the hall."

"Perhaps I am," she conceded. "But when Lord Carstairs assured Mr Fancot of his mother's good health last evening at dinner, and said that he had enjoyed one of the finest almond tarts he had ever tasted, I could have sworn I heard her mutter something under her breath."

"Indeed? And what might that have been?"

"I did not catch it all, but I am sure she said, 'pretty face'. It occurred to me that for all her bluster, Lady Carstairs might not be as confident as she appears. She once said to me, with some regret, that she had never been beautiful."

"You think she is jealous?" he said, surprised. "But Lord Carstairs is always very attentive to her, even flirtatious after all these years."

"I know," she agreed. "And I find it charming. I think he likes to reassure her of his affection, as if he senses that she still sometimes doubts it."

He did not look convinced, but at dinner that evening, Lady Carstairs saw that her husband was pushing his food around his plate rather than eating it and suddenly said, "Have you found some fault with the lamb, Carstairs? Or have you indulged yourself with so much of Mrs Fancot's almond tart that you have no room for it?"

Lord Seymore glanced across at Miss Hayes and they exchanged a meaningful look.

"You have found me out, my dear," he said gently. "I always have had a sweet tooth."

"Well you should know better," she said shortly. "You know full well that too many sweetmeats do not agree with you."

"You are, as usual, correct," he said, a little testily. "But it would be rude to refuse when she made it especially for me."

Lady Carstairs opened her mouth to no doubt utter one of her scathing comments, but he held up his hand and she closed it again. "If you will all excuse me," he said, getting to his feet. "I am going to lie down."

Lady Carstairs at once looked contrite. She also got to her feet. "You are ill, Carstairs. I will come with you."

He waved her away. "No, my dear. It is only a bilious stomach. I am sure that although I will no doubt suffer an uncomfortable night, I will find myself fully restored by the morning."

She sank back into her chair and said with unusual formality. "Very well, sir."

Once he had left the room, she turned her gaze upon Mr Fancot. "Do you not think it is time that you made your peace with your mother?"

He squirmed a little in his chair. "Perhaps, ma'am. I did not realise that Lord Carstairs would put himself to so much trouble. I cannot explain it to you, it is most awkward—"

"I do not wish for you to explain it to me, young man. I only wish that my husband is not put to so much trouble. I do not say that you should move back in with Mrs Fancot, for it is only right that you take your place here, but I would be very grateful if you would take it upon yourself to visit her in his stead."

Mr Fancot sent her a slightly resentful look, but only said, "I will certainly do so. But I am to go to Filton the day after tomorrow."

Lady Carstairs frowned "Must you go?"

"Yes, ma'am. I must. But I will only be gone a few days."

With that she had to be satisfied. "Very well. But once you return I expect you to relieve Lord Carstairs of this particular obligation."

CHAPTER 11

Harmony was restored the following morning. Lord Carstairs strolled into the breakfast parlour, his health and good humour seemingly restored. He went straight to his lady, took her hand, and dropped a light kiss upon it.

"Forgive me, my love, if I was a little crusty last evening."

"You are better then?" she said, giving him a close scrutiny.

"As you see," he smiled. "And I shall find a way to slip Mrs Fancot's tart into my pocket to-day. I am sure the birds will be very grateful for it. But I must ask you to take my place for a few days from tomorrow. I have decided to go to

Filton with Charles. I have discovered that it his birthday on Friday, and it would be a shame if he had no one to raise a glass with him."

"Of course," Lady Carstairs said, her rather pensive mood lifting. "I shall take her some cuttings for her garden."

"Will you be back in time for the ball?" Charlotte asked.

"I am afraid not, my child," he said gently. "I am very sorry to miss your first ball, but there will be many others, after all."

Sarah glanced up at her charge, expecting to see a look of disappointment upon her face. But instead, she saw a speculative gleam brighten her eyes.

"It is a shame," Charlotte said. "But perhaps you and my aunt would join us for our dancing lessons today? Chairs are all very well, but they do have their limitations. Sir Horace really needs to practice having to move around, and interact with, other dancers."

Lords Carstairs looked at his lady and raised a questioning brow.

"Is it safe?" Lady Carstairs said dryly.

Sir Horace laughed. "If you had asked me that question only two days ago, ma'am, I would have replied most definitely not. I still cannot guarantee it, but I am hopeful you may escape unscathed."

Her eyes turned back to her husband. "I think we might risk it, Carstairs."

Charlotte's eyes now turned to her cousin. "I will need you too, Justin" she informed him firmly.

"As you wish," he said.

Sarah was pleased, although a little confounded, when Charlotte looked down the table at Mr Fancot, who was quietly eating his breakfast and said, "And I would be very happy if you too would join us, sir."

Whatever did she have in mind? Surely she did not expect the gentlemen to dance together?

Mr Fancot looked up in surprise. He had taken Sarah's advice very much to heart and kept his interactions with Charlotte to a minimum. "Thank you, but no. I have a dozen or more loose ends to tie up before I leave tomorrow."

"Please, Mr Fancot," she said coaxingly. "I have invited Miss Truboot to join us. That will make eight of us for the cotillion."

"Come along, Charles," said Lord Carstairs. "I am sure those loose ends can wait. Besides, didn't I tell you that you should be socialising more?"

Charlotte turned to her aunt. "I hope you do not mind that I took the liberty of inviting Miss Truboot without your permission."

"No, why should I mind? Did I not tell you to spread your wings? Glad you're making friends." She suddenly frowned. "I wonder if she will bring her mother?"

"I expect she will be too busy making the arrangements for this evening's dinner," Charlotte said soothingly.

"I hope you are right, dear. She is a most encroaching woman, although I see nothing to object to in her daughter. She has very pretty manners; must take after her father."

"But, Charlotte," Sarah said, 'there will only be eight of us if I join in. But then who will play?"

"Mr Bamber," she said, looking very pleased with herself. "I discovered that he plays the violin when he came to dinner. I sent a note to him yesterday, asking if he would accompany us." She sent a laughing look at Sir Horace. "He replied that he had always wished to see a miracle, and would not miss it for the world!"

"Did he, by Jove?" said Sir Horace. "Fully expects me to fall flat on my face, no doubt. But I will say this for him, he's a fine fiddle player."

"You have been very sly, Charlotte Fletcher," Lady Carstairs said. "No, do not look downcast. Glad to see you've got so much initiative, and I have nothing at all to say against your plan. But I can't help wondering why you felt it necessary to spring it upon us like this. It might have fallen sadly flat, after all, if we had all refused."

"I did not want Sir Horace to worry," she said, flushing. "I know what it is like to lie awake at night, worrying about some silly little thing that is to occur the next day. But I could not take anyone else into my confidence, or I would feel like I was going behind his back. It would have seemed as if we were all ganging up on him. I thought it better to ambush you all at the same time."

"I say, that's dashed thoughtful of you, Miss Fletcher," Sir Horace said, clearly touched by her consideration. "But I wouldn't have, you know. Worried, I mean. I think it an excellent notion. If I'm going to make a fool of myself, I'd rather do it here than in the ballroom."

"You won't," Charlotte said confidently.

"Very well," said Lady Carstairs, looking from one to the other. "Now, if you have quite finished organising us all, Charlotte, I suggest we meet in an hour. I refuse to do any form of exercise immediately after eating. It is very bad for the digestion."

"Inviting Mr Fancot was very well done of you, Charlotte," Sarah said approvingly as they moved chairs and occasional tables to make room for the dancing.

"I felt very sorry for him last night," she said. "I think my aunt was worried about Uncle Oliver and it made her sharper than usual. When she turned on poor Mr Fancot, he looked quite miserable."

"He no longer frightens you?"

"No. I think I may have overreacted," she admitted.

They turned as Riddle announced Miss Truboot.

Seeing that she looked a little uncomfortable, Charlotte rushed forwards and took her hands.

"Miss Truboot, I am so glad you could come."

"It was very kind of you to invite me, Miss Fletcher," she said shyly. "Mama is very pleased that I should have an opportunity to practice my dancing."

"But are *you*?" Charlotte said gently, recognising the anxiety in her eyes.

"Oh yes, but to be amongst so many strangers is a little daunting."

"I know exactly how you feel," Charlotte sympathised. "But you are not a complete stranger to Lord and Lady Carstairs, and you must have seen Mr Fancot at church, surely?"

"Yes, although I have hardly spoken to him. And I came with Mama when she paid Lady Carstairs a call."

Charlotte leaned forwards and whispered, "Do not worry, her bark is worse than her bite!"

Miss Truboot was surprised into a smile.

"That is better. You have no need to fear," Charlotte assured her. "The vicar is going to play for us, and he cannot be a stranger. Apart from myself, that leaves only Lord Seymore, my guardian, who is a very easygoing gentleman, and Sir Horace, who is a dear. Oh, and of course my companion, Miss Hayes."

Sarah came forwards and smiled at the girl. "And I am no dragon, I assure you."

"Oh, no, of course not," she murmured, colouring.

"I shall leave you two to get acquainted for a few minutes whilst I ask the footman to let it be known that we are almost ready."

By the time she returned they were sat with their heads together. Smiling, she went over to the pianoforte to find the music they would need. She had barely laid the sheets upon the music stand that Riddle had dug out from some-where when Mr Bamber was shown into the room. After throwing a rather casual greeting at the girls, he strode over to Sarah and bowed.

"Miss Hayes. I cannot tell you how much I am looking forwards to this," he said, laying his violin case upon the pianoforte and opening it.

"I hope that is because you are looking for-ward to celebrating your brother's success, sir."

He gave his rather wolfish grin. "I have al-ways been an optimist, ma'am."

As he tuned up his instrument, the others trickled into the room. Charlotte brought Miss Truboot to Mr Fancot and Lord Seymore came over to Sarah.

"I must warn you, ma'am, that it is your toes that might be in danger. My dancing is a little rusty."

She laughed. "Well, as you entrusted your horses to me, the least I can do is entrust my toes to you."

She watched, fascinated, as his eyes turned an even deeper shade of blue. They reminded her of the sky at dusk, just before the darkness claimed it. She blinked as Mr Bamber suddenly launched into the introduction of the dance and everyone hurriedly took their places.

Charlotte's little dancing party was an unqualified success. Not only did Sir Horace successfully negotiate the country dance, but his timing was so much improved, he even managed the more elaborate footwork required for the cotillion without once inconveniencing anyone else. Of all the dancers, Mr Fancot and Miss Truboot were the least accomplished, but they supported each other with understanding, bashful smiles, and by the time the vicar played the closing bars of the cotillion, they seemed quite comfortable with each other.

Charlotte beamed proudly at Sir Horace. "You did it! I knew you would."

Mr Bamber laid down his violin and came to shake his brother's hand. "Well done, Horace. You have improved beyond all recognition."

"Very good of you to say so, Loftus. But the credit lies at Miss Fletcher's door. She has the patience of a saint!"

The vicar bowed to her. "You have indeed wrought a minor miracle, Miss Fletcher."

She smiled. "I will not own to it. There was really nothing wrong with Sir Horace's dancing, it was only his timing that was out."

"Mind you," said Sir Horace. "I still haven't managed to hold a conversation at the same time."

"Probably just as well," Lady Carstairs said dryly.

Charlotte looked a little dismayed but relaxed when Sir Horace winked at her and grinned.

"I for one am quite fagged and will go and lie down," she continued. "I suggest you do the same Carstairs, you are looking a little peaky. It's hardly surprising as I suspect you were up half the night."

The Truboots lived in a modest manor house near the hamlet of Tincleton. Sarah and Charlotte shared the carriage with Lord and Lady Carstairs, Lord Seymore and Sir Horace followed in the curricle, and Mr Fancot brought up the rear. As their destination lay only three miles distant from Priddleton Hall, the journey was accomplished in a little under half an hour.

As they pulled up in front of the house, Lady Carstairs turned to her lord and said, "I shall be very interested to see whom they have managed to dredge up on such short notice, for I'll go bail Lady Truboot had no intention of holding a dinner tonight."

"Sheath your claws, my dear," he said gently. "I am sure she has gone to a great deal of trouble and expense on our behalf."

"I like Miss Truboot," Charlotte said quietly.

"She does seem a pleasant girl," conceded Lady Carstairs. "And I have no doubt she will be very grateful for your company tonight."

When they were shown into the drawing room, Lady Truboot rushed forwards, an apologetic smile on her face.

"I'm afraid that we have had a few cancellations. But I'm sure it cannot signify. I always think a smaller, more intimate gathering so much more enjoyable. And I am sure, if only you do not despise our plain fare, you will enjoy a very pleasant dinner." Her gaze rapidly scanned the company and alighted on Sarah. "Oh, I am so pleased that you bought Miss Fletcher's companion. I could not recall if I had made it clear that she was included in the invitation, and we have need of her to even up the numbers."

"I would not have dreamt of leaving her behind," Lady Carstairs said coolly. "Miss Hayes' grandfather, *Baron* Beaumont, was an old friend of mine," she added, not hesitating to stretch the truth a little.

"Oh, I see, that explains why she is dressed so finely." Lady Truboot turned back to Sarah and for the first time addressed her directly. "You are very welcome, Miss Hayes, I assure you."

Sarah could readily believe it when she had the opportunity to observe the other guests. The local squire, Mr Snook, who had ruddy cheeks and a bluff, forthright manner, seemed to delight in engaging in heated discussion with the equally forthright Lady Crossington. This lady, a formidable dowager of advanced years, had eyes as sharp as Lady Carstairs', and a tongue not softened by modern notions of politeness. The other guests, Mr and Mrs Moseley, were as quiet as the other two were loud, and did not seem to have any conversation at all.

Sarah found herself seated next to Mr Moseley at dinner. His narrow, weaselly eyes lit up as he surveyed the heavily laden table, and once he had exchanged a brief greeting with her, he enjoyed a hearty dinner, only occasionally remembering to serve her any of the tempting viands on offer.

This was a far more lavish affair than any served up at the hall. Lady Truboot's notions of plain fare would have satisfied the Prince Regent himself. She had indeed gone to much expense and trouble. The pea soup was followed by a myriad of dishes from lamb cutlets, green goose, dressed crabs and baked carp, to veal, beef-steaks, fricassee of chicken, and ducklings. A raised partridge pie, roasted fowl, pastries, creams, and jellies followed.

Only Sir Horace broke the strict etiquette of the occasion. So moved was he by the feast set before him, he suddenly exclaimed, "Devilish fine food, ma'am. My compliments to your chef."

A chorus of approval followed. Lady Truboot looked a little relieved, Sarah thought. Perhaps she had noticed that Lord Carstairs was only picking at his food. But judging by the frequent glances she sent in the direction of her daughter and Mr Fancot, this was not her prime concern.

When the ladies left the gentlemen to their port, Lady Crossington turned her penetrating gaze upon Lady Truboot. "That was indeed a most excellent, if rather extravagant dinner, ma'am. I only hope you recoup your investment."

Lady Truboot's ample bosom swelled. "I do not know what you mean, Lady Crossington. If my guests have enjoyed their repast, then I must be satisfied, I am sure."

"Of that, at least, you may be certain," she said.

She turned her attention to Sarah. "Did I hear you are related to old Berty Beaumont, Miss Hayes?"

"Yes, ma'am. It was through my grandfather that I first met Lady Carstairs, when he took me to visit Lady Brabacombe."

She was aware of a feeling of relief when those piercing eyes turned in Lady Carstairs' direction. She had no wish to suffer a close interrogation of her family history and she was quite sure that Lady Crossington would not hesitate to subject her to one if she felt so inclined.

"You knew Letty Brabacombe?" she said.

"I doubt anyone knew her better," Lady Carstairs said. "I lived with her for fifteen years!"

"Really? If you survived such an ordeal unscathed, you must be made of stern stuff. We were arch rivals at one time. We enjoyed many a spat," she said reminiscently. "I've always preferred a worthy enemy to a fawning friend."

"I would imagine that is a fortunate circumstance," Lady Carstairs said dryly.

Lady Truboot gasped and Mrs Moseley seemed to shrink in her chair. But it seemed to Sarah that they were cast from the same mould, so she was not surprised when Lady Crossington gave a bark of laugher and invited Lady Carstairs to sit with her.

Charlotte and Miss Truboot had moved a little apart and were talking in hushed whispers. Lady Truboot glanced from one couple to the other and then placed herself halfway between them.

Sarah turned to Mrs Moseley, determined to draw her out.

"Had you far to come, ma'am?"

The lady smiled a little nervously. "Oh, no."

"We are fortunate that the weather has remained fine."

"Yes, indeed."

"It was a fine dinner, was it not?"

"Oh, I quite agree."

Many awkward silences accompanied their stilted conversation and she was extremely grateful when the gentlemen finally joined them. Her eyes seemed to find Lord Seymore's of their own accord. He raised a brow and moved towards her, but Sir Richard was before him.

"I am very pleased to make your acquaintance, ma'am. I knew your mother once upon a time. Your hair is your father's, but your eyes and your smile are hers."

It seemed she was not to escape a discussion of her family after all.

"I hardly knew her, sir," she admitted. "I was very young when she died."

"It is such a pity she was taken so soon," he said softly. "She was vivacious and bright, yet gentle and kind."

"It seems you knew her well. I envy you."

"Yes, I did." He leaned a little towards her and said, "Just between you and me, Miss Hayes, I asked her to be my wife. But she had eyes only for your father."

"Sir Richard!" called Lady Truboot.

He winced as her piercing voice rose above the quiet hubbub of conversation.

"Come and lend your voice to mine. Lord Carstairs says he must be going soon as he has an early start in the morning, but the night is yet young."

He sent Sarah an apologetic glance and obeyed his wife's summons. She hardly had a moment to recover from this revelation when Mr Snook slipped into the spot vacated by Sir Richard.

Having enjoyed a gargantuan supper and liberal potations of port and brandy, he was in a mellow and rather jolly mood. His naturally ruddy complexion had brightened to the hue of a ripe tomato. Sarah suspected he might be a trifle disguised and she was certain of it when he squeezed her hand and said, "Been hoping to have a word with you all evening, Miss Hayes. Never seen such a fine looking woman!"

As she did not know how to answer this, she was relieved when Lady Crossington's biting tones snapped across the room. "Stop molesting that poor girl, Snook, and come and persuade Lady Carstairs that the Dorchester summer fair is worth attending."

"Curse the woman!" he muttered under his breath. He reluctantly released Sarah's hand. "Don't go anywhere, will you? Shouldn't be above a few minutes."

Lord Seymore approached her, a satirical gleam in his eye.

"You look a little subdued, Miss Hayes. I am at a loss to understand it. Have you not found the company congenial?"

Sarah laughed. "Mr Snook is rather too congenial, and if you had spent most of your evening with Mr and Mrs Moseley, you would not ask. I wonder if they even speak to each other when they are at home!"

"I wonder which is worse," he pondered, "sitting next to someone who never speaks, or being saddled with someone who slips some very probing questions between a plethora of incon-sequential small talk."

"I have, at least, been saved from those probing questions," she said. "Lady Truboot has been too busy trying to eavesdrop on everyone else's conversation."

"I think Lady Truboot will be very pleased with her evening's work," he said.

Sarah followed his gaze and saw that Mr Fancot, Miss Truboot, Charlotte, and Sir Horace had formed a little group. Miss Truboot was smiling and shaking her head at something Mr Fancot was saying to her.

"Yes, perhaps," she acknowledged. "I believe it is not uncommon for a young man to fall out of love with one young lady only to tumble headlong in love with another."

"When the apple is ripe, it will fall," he said. "And it is not at all uncommon when the young man is inexperienced, and if it was only a case of infatuation. As Charlotte was the first pretty young female Mr Fancot had had any great ex-posure to, it is quite understandable that he might have mistaken his feelings."

Sarah looked a little downcast. "You are right, of course. It is a lowering thought, but I have accepted that I am quite over the hill."

He laughed. "Don't talk such nonsense. You

are a diamond of the first water, as well you know! But I think Mr Fancot's tastes run to more shy, retiring young ladies."

"Yes," she said mournfully. "And I fear he thinks I am something of a bluestocking."

"Not to mention being an out and outer in the saddle and a fine whip to boot!"

"Indeed, it needed only that. I can quite see that he must find me a quite shocking female."

He smiled down at her in a most disturbing way. "I think he probably does, Miss Hayes."

It was on the tip of her tongue to ask him if he found her so, and she was grateful that Lady Carstairs chose that moment to take her leave. Somehow she had slipped into her old way of funning, and it would have seemed as if she were fishing for compliments.

"Surely you do not all need to go?" Lady Truboot said, a little desperately.

"I suppose not," Lady Carstairs said. "Charlotte and Miss Hayes will come with us, of course. But the others may do as they wish."

Sir Percy exchanged a look with Lord Seymore. "I think Seymore and I should act as escort, you know. Dashed dark night, might be highwaymen lurking about. Never can tell."

Lady Crossington sniggered.

"I will stay a little longer, ma'am," Mr Fancot said quietly.

Lady Truboot's equilibrium was immediately restored.

"Well," Lady Carstairs said, once they were in the carriage. "That evening proved far more entertaining than I had bargained for."

"I am glad you found it so," Lord Carstairs said, a little wearily. "I think you too enjoyed it, Charlotte."

"Oh yes. Emma and I had many ideas in common."

He smiled across at Sarah.

"I do not think you found it quite so amusing, Miss Hayes."

"Who were those people?" she asked.

"I assume you are referring to Mr and Mrs Moseley as you seemed to be burdened with them for most of the evening?"

"Yes. I have never met people with so little to say for themselves."

"Mr Moseley used to be involved in banking, I believe," he said. "He was rather more expansive when you ladies left the room. From one or two comments he dropped, which do not bear repeating, I gather he is not overly fond of female company."

"Poor Mrs Moseley," Sarah said.

"Precisely," agreed Lord Carstairs.

As they made their way to bed, Lady Carstairs said, "Come to my room for a few minutes, will you, Carstairs? There is something I wish to discuss with you and I may not get the opportunity in the morning."

CHAPTER 12

Lord Seymore and Sir Horace were not yet ready for their beds and made their way to the library for a nightcap.

"I say, that was a very pleasant evening," Sir Horace said, as he sipped a glass of Lord Carstairs' fine claret.

Lord Seymore grinned. "I suspect, my friend, that you would think anywhere my ward happened to be, pleasant."

"And why wouldn't I?" he said. "She's a very pleasant girl."

"Yes," he agreed. "She is a credit to me."

Sir Horace gave him a stern look. "But that is no thanks to you, is it? It is fortunate that her good nature has remained intact after you all but abandoned her."

Lord Seymore looked a little startled. "Did she say that?"

"Of course she didn't. Seems to think the world of you, but why she should is beyond me. Claims she was very happy at the seminary, but I can read between the lines, and I'd say there have been times when she's been dashed lonely. It's not what I'd have wanted for my sister. If it wasn't for Miss Hayes, I shudder to think what might have happened to her. Don't bear thinking about."

"I am fully aware of the debt I owe Miss Hayes,' Lord Seymore said, a little testily. "It is because of Miss Hayes that I allowed her to remain at the school, but you may be sure I would have removed her if she had seemed unhappy. I did invite her to Winbourne you know. She didn't want to come."

"Hardly surprising," he said. "A person knows when they're not wanted."

Lord Seymore frowned down at his glass. Sir Horace's barb had shot home. Although he would have done his duty if necessary, he had not wanted such a complication in his life.

"Sorry, old chap," his friend said in a bewildered voice. "Don't know what came over me. Not my place to say anything. Tell you what you should have done though."

Lord Seymore smiled wryly. "I'm all ears, Bamber."

"You should have got yourself a wife; given the girl a mother. Come to think of it, still should. Seems to me, Lord Carstairs ain't in the best of health, and Lady Carstairs won't enjoy all the fuss and botheration of Town, besides, she'll scare off all but the most determined of fellows. Find a wife, Seymore, and let her bring Miss Fletcher out."

"I was hoping that would not be necessary," he murmured.

"Not necessary? The girl's got to make her come out!"

"I thought you might have an interest in Miss Fletcher," Lord Seymore said gently.

Sir Horace's eyes widened to their fullest extent. "Now just wait a minute, Seymore. Very fond of her, I'm sure, just like I'm fond of my sister. But a man don't want to marry his sister!"

The butler came into the room, looking slightly displeased.

Lord Seymore smiled apologetically at him. "Are we keeping you up, Riddle?"

"Not at all, sir. Mr Fancot has not yet come in. I am afraid there was a little mix-up this morning. A letter came for you but it was delivered to Lord Carstairs with the rest of his mail. I did not have a chance to give it to you before you went out."

Lord Seymore took it from him. "Thank you. Do not let it trouble you. I doubt it is anything of any moment."

As Riddle left the room, he scanned its contents, and then read it again more slowly.

"Nothing amiss, I hope, Seymore?"

He looked up. "I cannot tell. My neighbour, Sir Francis Hopton, says he has something he wishes to say to me. Says it cannot wait. He's invited me to dinner, tomorrow."

"Seems an impatient sort of chap. Will you go?"

"I rather think I will. He is a very mild-mannered man, and for him to have written to me when he knows I am engaged elsewhere, suggests it is a matter of some importance."

"But you will miss the ball! Miss Fletcher's first ball! You're her guardian. Got to come."

"I may still make it. It should only take me seven hours, six if I push it, to reach Winbourne. Unless something unforeseen prevents me, I should be back in time. But don't wait for me if I am delayed; take Lord Carstairs' place in the carriage and I will meet you there. But watch over Charlotte in my stead, will you?"

Sir Horace got to his feet and yawned. "Be

my pleasure to. But do try to make it if you can, old fellow. It's time you started taking your obligations seriously." He shook his head. "There I go again, sermonising. Don't understand it. Not like me at all."

Lord Seymore smiled. "You have imbibed a potent mix of wine, port, and brandy, this evening, Bamber. It has loosened your tongue in a most alarming manner."

"That must be it," Sir Horace said. "No offence meant, old chap."

"And none taken. Now take yourself to bed before you fall asleep where you stand."

"Yes, I think I will. Night, Seymore."

"Goodnight, Bamber."

Lord Seymore gently swirled the dregs of his wine and looked down into them with a concentrated gaze, much as a fortune teller might intently try and read the tea leaves. Sometime later, he sighed and set it carefully down. He made his way to bed, but it was a long time before sleep claimed him.

His valet woke him promptly at six o'clock. He arose rather groggily and slipped his arms into the dressing gown Tench held ready for him. Crossing to his washstand, he splashed several handfuls of warm water over his face in an effort to clear his head.

"Heavy night was it, sir?"

"Something like that," murmured Lord Seymore.

"Better let me shave you this morning then," he said, running the blade of the razor along the strop.

It was a task Lord Seymore usually preferred to do himself, but this morning he allowed his valet to have his way whilst he pondered why Sir Francis needed to see him so urgently. But by the time his square jaw was smooth once more, he was no nearer an answer.

"I've packed your overnight bag, sir. You did say it was only one night we'd be away?"

"I hope so, Tench. But I won't be needing you."

Tench had been cleaning the razor; he winced as he nicked his finger.

"I am glad that I waited until you had finished shaving me to mention it," Lord Seymore murmured.

"But, sir, you are dining with Sir Francis and Lady Hopton. Who will dress you?"

He laughed. "I think you will find I can manage. I must have dined with them a hundred times, and we are on such good terms that I cannot imagine they will raise a brow if my boots do not shine quite so brightly as usual."

Tench frowned. "I've already polished your boots, sir. They'll find no fault with them. But who will press your coat?"

"I'm sure I have a dozen pressed coats at Winbourne. Now stop fussing, man. I will hear no more. I will be in a hurry to change for the ball when I return and need you to have all my clothes laid out, ready."

"Of course, my lord."

Lord Seymore knew he had deeply offended his valet when he addressed him in such formal, frigid tones.

"If it will make you feel any better," he said, torn between amusement and exasperation, "I will wear whatever you choose without a word of complaint."

He saw his valet's eyes brighten and wished he could recall his rash words, but he had no more time to waste. By the time he was dressed and had gulped down his coffee, it was almost seven o'clock. He hurried down to the stables. It was not his curricle that waited in the yard, however, but Lord Carstairs'. That gentleman was seated in his vehicle with the reins in his hands.

"Good morning, sir," he said, striding up to him.

"It is a fine morning for a journey, Seymore.

Riddle informs me that you are off to Winbourne."

"Yes, sir. But I hope to be away for one night only."

"Matter of business?"

"Yes, sir."

"Then you must, of course, go. Be back for the ball?"

"That is my intention," he confirmed.

"Good. Charlotte would be disappointed if you missed it."

Mr Fancot rushed across the cobbles, a basket in his hand.

"I am sorry to have kept you waiting, sir," he said with a wry smile. "I overslept a little and then Mrs Baines would not let me leave before she had prepared this basket. I told her the housekeeper at Filton was expecting us and we would be there by noon, but she does not seem to think we can survive that long without suste-nance. She says you can't trust the muck they serve up at coaching inns!"

"I am sure we shall be very grateful for it," Lord Carstairs said gently.

Mr Fancot placed it on the floor of the curri-cle, but hesitated with his foot on the step. "Are you sure you do not wish me to drive, sir?"

"Quite sure," said Lord Carstairs firmly. "I

was driving long before you were born young man, and I wouldn't be surprised if I could teach you a thing or two."

Mr Fancot grinned and climbed aboard. "I shall look forward to it, sir."

Lord Seymore waved them off but they had to pull up sharply to avoid colliding with Mrs Baines as she rushed into the yard, something wrapped in fine muslin clutched in her hands.

"I'm glad I caught you, sir," she said, gasping. "Mrs Fancot just sent this almond tart up from the dower house. Apparently it's a great favourite of yours. Said perhaps she wouldn't be quite forgotten whilst you were away if you took it."

Mr Fancot took it from her and added it to the basket.

"Send her my thanks, will you?" Lord Carstairs said, as they moved off.

Lord Seymore looked after them thoughtfully. Could it be that Lady Carstairs had a reason to be jealous? No, he could not believe it. It was far more likely that the message was meant for her son.

He made good time, and even with a brief stop for some refreshment, he reached Winbourne by two o'clock. He smiled as he saw the red-bricked mansion in the distance. It was built upon the foundations of a thirteenth century monastery, but had been remodelled in the Palladian style. The only clues to its ancient origins were the cloistered courtyard and the cellarium that lay beneath it.

He had expected to take his housekeeper and butler by surprise, having had no time to send them warning of his arrival, but when he strolled into the hall, Skelforth was waiting for him.

"You made very good time, sir," he said, relieving Lord Seymore of his hat and greatcoat.

He looked at him in some surprise. "Have you developed the gift of foresight, Skelforth?"

"I only wish I had, sir," he said with the ghost of a smile. "How useful it would be."

Before he could reply, Mrs Norton, his housekeeper, issued from the door that led down to the kitchens and her sitting room.

"My lord, I did not expect you quite so early. You must have been driving at breakneck speed," she said, in the reproving tones only a retainer of very long standing would have dared to use.

"No," he assured her. "I may have sprung the horses a little, but not excessively, I assure you."

"If you say so, sir," she said. "But you needn't worry; you will find all in readiness."

He smiled at her. "Of that I am in no doubt, Mrs Norton. But what I would like to know, is how you knew to expect me at all?"

"Miss Hopton came over, must have been about an hour ago. Hoped to have a word with you before you went over to Shaldon for dinner."

"Did she now?" he said.

"Yes, sir. Seemed most anxious to speak with you. If it had been any other young lady come a calling, I would have sent her away with a flea in her ear, you may be sure. But seeing as you and Miss Hopton have been firm friends this many a year, I just told her kindly, that if Sir Francis had only written to you two days ago, it was most unlikely that you would be here for a few hours yet."

"I see," he said, although, if truth be told, he did not see at all. What the deuce was going on?

Knowing that Sir Francis liked to dine at five o'clock, he arrived at a quarter past four, hoping for a quiet word with Miss Hopton. This opportunity was not granted him, however. The butler showed him immediately into the study.

Sir Francis was seated behind his desk, but

immediately got to his feet and came forwards to greet his guest.

"Seymore, I knew you would not fail me," he said, shaking his hand warmly.

Lord Seymore glanced down into the genial countenance of his host, but did not fail to note the slightly harassed expression in his eyes.

"Of course I would not, sir. I do not know what has occasioned this summons, but you may be sure I will help you if I can."

Sir Francis's hand was still lost within Lord Seymore's far larger one, but he placed his other over it and said, "I know, Seymore, I know. Please take a seat."

He nodded to his butler and he poured two glasses of wine, and then left them.

"There's been some more trouble at the salt pans, Seymore. You did very well to withdraw your investment, last year. This salt tax is killing the industry."

"That is why I put my money into the boat-yard, sir."

"Yes. And a very good thing you did too," Sir Francis said. "Unfortunately, it has also en-couraged the smugglers to take an interest."

Lord Seymore nodded. "It was only a matter of time. The tax is unsustainable and there is very little, if any, profit to be made."

"Indeed. But unfortunately, we have a very earnest salt officer, a Mr Fawlty, who is determined to make his name and bring the culprits to justice. The trouble is, his dedication to his duty is not matched by any degree of restraint or sense. He has put two and two together and made five."

"I fear you will have to elucidate a little more if you wish me to understand you, sir," Lord Seymore said.

"He seems to think it is very interesting that the production, and therefore the tax paid, fell off substantially not long after you withdrew your interest. When he discovered, by what means I know not, that an extensive cellarium runs beneath your house, and the river that flows through your lands joins the sea at Lymington, he came to the erroneous assumption that it would be the perfect place to store the undeclared surplus until it was time to ship it out. He has applied to me, as the local magistrate, for permission to search your property for the proof he sorely needs."

"But, sir, was it really necessary to call me back on this fool's errand? Surely you know the Seymore's have never colluded with the smugglers? My father was never in sympathy with them."

Sir Francis nodded. "I know, I know. But the wars have cost the government a great deal, and they need to recoup their money where they can. This bumptious upstart, has persuaded certain influential people of the justness of his cause."

Lord Seymore frowned. "Let him search. I have nothing to hide. Although I am still at a loss to understand the urgency; I had intended to return in another week or so, anyway."

Sir Francis took a thoughtful sip of his wine. "Yes, well, you will me doing me a great service if you can remove this thorn from my side."

Lord Seymore's expression lightened. "Is he that bad, sir?"

Sir Francis laughed. "He is like an irritating wasp, who circles about you incessantly."

"Then it will be my pleasure to remove his sting, sir," Lord Seymore said, smiling.

"You are a credit to your father, Seymore," Sir Francis said, a little gruffly. "I still miss him you know."

"Yes, I know you were great friends, sir. I miss him too. Winbourne is not the same without him."

Lord Seymore found himself on the end of a suddenly keen stare. "No. I am sure it is not. It is time you put your own stamp upon it, Seymore.

You need to install a wife there and set up your nursery."

"Yes. I have been considering it, sir."

"Capital. That brings me to the other reason I sent for you."

"Oh?"

"I have been approached by a respectable gentleman, a Mr Clayton. Do you know him?"

"I do not believe I do."

"No, well you have been much occupied of late. He is a very respectable gentleman and is the second son of the Earl of Frome. He has fortunately not suffered the destiny of so many younger sons, but has been gifted his estate at Pennington, some ten miles from here. It is of a reasonable size, and if managed well, should provide a comfortable income."

"I am glad to hear it, sir. But I do not quite see what this has to do with me."

Sir Francis shifted a little in his chair. "Can it be unknown to you, that your father and I hoped you might bind the ties that have always bound our families together, a little tighter?"

Lord Seymore did not pretend to misunderstand him. "You mean Lucy, I suppose."

"I do," he said. "You two have always been good friends and I was content to wait. But she is now four and twenty, Seymore, almost upon the shelf, you might say. Mr Clayton has made an appointment to see me tomorrow. He has paid Lucy a flattering degree of attention since he met her at a ball in Lymington a month ago, so I fancy I know why he comes."

"I see," Lord Seymore said thoughtfully. "And you think Lucy will accept his offer?"

"There is only one possible reason why she might not. She likes him well enough, but not as much as she likes you, I suspect."

"Now I understand your urgency, sir."

"Yes, I wished to give you an opportunity to consider your future before I met with Mr Clayton."

Lord Seymore felt a little irritated. Although Lucy had been at the top of his short list of prospective brides, he did not like to be hurried into a decision in this way.

"I suggest you take her for a walk in the garden after dinner, and have some private conversation with her. But whatever you decide, you will always be welcome at Shaldon as I hope you know. Now, I think we should join the ladies."

He had barely stepped foot inside the drawing room when a slightly plump lady with a kindly face came towards him, her hands outstretched.

"Justin. How lovely it is to see you."

He took the hands offered to him and dropped a kiss on Lady Hopton's lightly powdered cheek.

"How are you, Lady Hopton?"

"I am very well, thank you." She gave him a close scrutiny. "I am not sure I can say the same about you, however. You look a little pale."

He smiled. "The result of a late night and an early start, ma'am."

"Well, never mind. A good dinner will set you to rights."

"Did you buy your chestnuts, Justin?" Miss Hopton said, coming forwards with her hand outstretched.

He took it and held it for a moment. "Indeed I did, Lucy. And I am very pleased with them."

"I take it then, that they are prime goers?"

He laughed. "Precisely."

Miss Hopton was not a beauty; her hair, like her mother's, was of an unremarkable brown, but there was something very pleasing about her regular features, the most distinguished of which was a pair of clear grey eyes.

"And how is your ward?" Lady Hopton enquired.

"Charlotte is very content with her great aunt," he said.

"I am very pleased to hear it. There can be

no need for you to run away again, for a few days, at least."

"As to that, ma'am. I am afraid I cannot stay above a night. Charlotte attends her first ball tomorrow. I would not wish to miss it."

"No, of course not," she said, a little regretfully.

At dinner, once they had exhausted the subject of the ridiculous salt officer, he was bombarded with questions about Priddleton Hall, the Carstairs, and all the other guests at present staying there. They enjoyed listening to Sir Horace's trials and tribulations very much, as they did the description of some of the characters at Lady Truboot's dinner.

"It seems to me, Justin," Lady Hopton said as he finished, "that Charlotte has more than enough protectors about her. Sir Horace appears to be quite smitten with her."

Lord Seymore smiled. "He is, indeed, ma'am, although he does not yet realise it."

"Yes, well, more than one gentlemen had been guilty of that, I'm sure." She let that hang in the air for a moment, and Lord Seymore glanced across at Lucy. She dropped her eyes and flushed.

"And Lady Carstairs sounds like a formidable woman."

"I cannot disagree," he said.

"And then there is Miss Hayes."

Lucy raised her eyes and he turned his own away. "Yes, ma'am. She is as a lioness guarding her cub."

"Yet you still feel it necessary to rush back to Priddleton Hall."

He did, he realised. "Charlotte expects it of me."

Lady Hopton gave him a searching look and then capitulated. "You have changed a little, I think, Justin. You are finally taking your duties seriously. It is well."

"I think we can forgo the port," Sir Francis said. "Take Lucy for an airing whilst the air is still warm."

Lord Seymore looked across at her again and she nodded, fiercely blushing. She knew what was in the wind, then. As she fetched her bonnet and pelisse, he strode up and down the hall, his brain working rapidly. Lucy had long been his confidant, she had often ridden or walked with him when his father was so ill. And all of the Hoptons had supported him after his death. When he had thought of taking a wife, Lucy had seemed like the perfect candidate; they had known each other since they were children. He suddenly recalled Sir Horace's words of the evening before, *a man don't want to marry his sister.* He did not for a moment believe that Sir Horace really regarded Charlotte as a sister, but he now realised that it was precisely how he regarded Lucy.

Yet judging by her blushes, his proposal would not be unwelcome. What was he to do? He had no wish to cause his childhood friend any pain, but he was not at all sure he could bring himself up to the mark.

He stopped pacing as Lucy ran lightly down the stairs, smiled, and offered her his arm.

"The rose garden?" he suggested.

She shook her head. "No, let us go into the park."

They walked in silence for some moments, the heavy weight of expectation between them. Finally, he could bear it no longer. He suddenly turned to her and took both of her hands in his. It was strange, she was not the blushing sort, yet here she was, her cheeks as crimson as the setting sun.

"Lucy. We have always been honest with each other, so let us be now. Do you wish to marry me?"

The blush faded as a gleam of amusement brightened her eyes. "Justin, you graceless creature! Was that meant as a proposal?"

"Yes. No. That is, I am merely trying to ascertain your feelings."

She laughed at his discomfort. "I believe the gentlemen is meant to screw his courage to the sticking place, not try and ascertain what his fair maiden is likely to answer before he asks her!"

He looked a little sheepish. "I am making a sad hash of it, aren't I?"

"Indeed, you are, my friend. I am going to ask you to trust me."

He brows winged up. "I do trust you, Lucy."

"Good. Now ask me."

He hesitated and she smiled. "Trust me." It was not her words but the gleam of mischief in her eyes that swung it.

"Lucy Hopton, will you marry me?" The words came out at speed and lacked conviction.

She laughed again. "That is a slight improvement, but it is still woeful. I am afraid I am left with no choice, Justin. I must decline your not so gracious offer."

He felt a weight lift from his shoulders. "Lucy! You wretch! Why did you not just tell me you did not wish to marry me at the outset!"

"I was going to," she assured him. "It is why I rushed over to Winbourne to try and see you earlier. I thought it would be a simple matter to speak of with you, and perhaps it would have been, but you were not there. My father spoke with me before you arrived, he seemed to think that you would wish for the match."

Lord Seymore smiled sympathetically. "And he probably laid it on thick that it was his and my father's long-held wish that we should tie the knot."

"Yes. That's exactly it. However it was, he put a seed of doubt into my mind."

Her eyes softened. "Justin, you are my dear, dear, friend, I would not wish to cause you any pain. I did not know what I was going to do. I felt quite mortified. But when you finally spoke, I could see you were as reluctant as I. We would have a very pleasant marriage, I am sure, but it would lack a certain something, don't you think?"

"Yes, dear Lucy. And I think you may have discovered that Mr Clayton has that certain something."

A gentle glow warmed her eyes. "Indeed, I have."

"Then I wish you very happy."

"Thank you."

"But why did you make me declare myself?"

"Because then neither mama or papa can lay the blame at your door, stoopid! You asked and I refused. You could have done no more."

He looked down at her fondly. "You need not have, you know. Your father has already assured me that I will always be welcome here whatever I chose to do."

"Well, now we can be certain of it."

They had been slowly walking towards the house. As they neared it, Lucy turned to him, stood on her tiptoes, and swiftly kissed his cheek. "Don't come in, Justin. Leave it to me to explain."

She ran up the steps to the front door and then looked over her shoulder, the mischief back in her eyes. "I think you may also have found someone with that certain something, Justin. I suggest you practise your address before you put your courage to the sticking place a second time."

She disappeared inside before he could answer.

CHAPTER 13

He drove back to Winbourne, deep in thought. But he was jolted from his ruminations as he drove up the avenue. A bright flash, as might be made when the sun reflects off glass, caught his attention. He slowed his horses and saw it again. It was some distance away, and came from a place where he knew there to be no windows. The river was near the spot, but it had deep banks and he could not, he knew, have seen the suns dying rays reflected on the water from here.

Skelforth had clearly been on the watch for him. The door opened before he had mounted the shallow steps that led to it. His butler's face was grave.

"There is a Mr Fawlty awaiting you in the green saloon, sir." Disapproval was etched into every syllable. "Apparently he works for the salt office and has some urgent business with you. I told him you were out, but he insisted that he would wait for you. None of my usual methods of persuasion have had any effect upon him, and short of bodily throwing him out – something I would have been sorely tempted to do if only I hadn't given footman John a few days leave to visit his family – there was very little I could do."

"I will see him, Skelforth," he said, passing him his hat. However, when the butler moved to help him out of his greatcoat, he shook his head. "Have you served him any refreshment?"

"No, sir."

"Good. You need not trouble yourself."

It appeared the time had come to rid Sir Francis of his annoying wasp. He threw open the door to the green saloon and stood a moment in the doorway, his stance wide and his many caped greatcoat making his shoulders so broad they all but touched the frame on each side. One eyebrow rose in a haughty manner any of his friends would have been astonished to see. The pugnacious little official, who had risen hastily to his feet, and had been, he was sure, about to issue a challenge, promptly closed his mouth and paled a little.

"Mr Fawlty?"

"That is correct, sir."

"It is an odd time to come calling, is it not? To what do I owe the pleasure?" he said coldly.

The rather slight little man made something of a recover. He drew himself up to his full height, tipped his head back, and looked down his long nose. As Mr Fawlty's head did not even reach Lord Seymore's shoulders, his narrowed gaze rested on the third button of Lord Seymore's greatcoat, somewhat ruining the effect.

"As you have been dining with Sir Francis this evening, I am sure you know what this is about, sir."

"You refer to the mountains of salt you believe to be stowed in my cellar, I presume."

He uttered these words with such scornful incredulity, that a look of uncertainty crossed Mr Fawlty's face, as if he were no longer quite so sure of his sagacity.

"I mean no offence, I am sure, sir—"

"Then what do you mean, man? You have applied, several times, I believe, for a warrant to search my house. A warrant, I would remind you, which you have not as yet been granted, armed only with the information that the profits from the salt pans fell dramatically not long after I had withdrawn my interest in the business—"

"The decline in profitability started long before that, sir."

"Which is why I decided to invest my money elsewhere," Lord Seymore said. "Not an unreasonable act, I think? You have aired your baseless suspicions in various quarters, thus calling the good name of my family into disrepute, and you have at least one man, and probably more, trespassing on my land by the river."

"Seeing as you had been alerted to my suspicions, I thought it better to take some precautions. And I admit I do not have a warrant to search your property as yet, something which in itself I find rather telling—"

"What it tells you, Mr Fawlty, is that Sir Francis has more integrity than to let you search a man's property when he isn't even there to witness the outrageous event."

Mr Fawlty's eyes narrowed even further. "Or perhaps, being as you're friends, he thought to warn you. It is well known that smuggling has had a grip on these parts for many a year, and if you mean to tell me that more than one fine gentleman is not involved in it in some way or other, whether it is turning a blind eye or accepting a delivery of brandy or wine——"

"I mean to tell you no such thing," Lord Seymore said calmly. "Only that my family has never done so."

This prosaic response rather deflated the head of steam Mr Fawlty had been building, but he did not lose sight of his objective. "Well then, sir," he said, his voice a little flat, clearly disappointed that he had not been able to lead up to his primary demand with any degree of drama, "if you have nothing to hide, surely you will not object to me looking in your cellars?"

Lord Seymore decided it was time to call an end to this farce.

"Mr Fawlty, I shall ask my butler to give you a tour of the cellarium. When you have finished, I would ask that you collect your men, leave my estate, and do not step foot upon it again. You have acted far beyond your remit and I would be well within my rights to raise a considerable fuss over this matter, but as I have to leave first thing in the morning, I shall on this occasion, refrain from doing so. You will have enough explaining to do as it is. You have made a great fool of yourself, Mr Fawlty, and when your superiors read your report, I fear your career will be in some jeopardy."

He registered the look of shifty unease on his uninvited guest's face with some satisfaction, turned on his heel, and left the room.

He found Skelforth lurking in the hallway. "Give him a few minutes to consider his folly and then show him the cellarium, will you?"

He retreated to his study, shed his greatcoat, and sank into an armchair. His lips twitched as he imagined the consternation that would surely grip Mr Fawlty when he realised how gross an error he had made.

Perhaps he should feel more sympathy for the man, for had not his own judgement also been at fault? He had thought he wished for a comfortable wife, who would not interfere overly with his manner of living, but this evening's events, had showed him how hollow such an existence would be.

Like Mr Fancot, he threw himself into the work of his estate, although unlike him, not to the exclusion of everything else. He had a wide circle of friends and was frequently invited to join them on some spree or other. At the end of a long day, he usually sat in this chair and felt quite content with his lot. But he was aware that he would have enjoyed having someone one to laugh with about the unfortunate salt officer's visit. Miss Hayes, for example, was always quick to enjoy the ridiculous.

Lucy had always been very perceptive. One of the things he had always liked most in her was her tacit understanding. He had not needed to explain things to her; she had always sensed when he was troubled and had not demanded or needed tedious explanations. She was right, of course, Miss Hayes had always had that certain something extra, and he had, on occasion, felt a similar connection to the one he had with Lucy, especially in matters of humour. The trouble was, he had no idea what she thought of him.

What he did know was that she had felt her position, last evening. Until she had been aware of her connections, Lady Truboot had treated her as a non-entity, and even then, had clearly not thought her worthy of any but the most minimal courtesy. In stark contrast, she had received some rather too warm attention from Mr Snook, and must have been fully alive to the fact that he would never have been so forward, no matter how bosky, if she had not been the hired help. She had turned it off with a wry smile, but he found it intolerable that a woman, who was far above so many of her sex in both accomplishments and beauty, should be subjected to such treatment.

Would the certain something that sparked between them make up for the disruption to his life? He was beginning to think that a few months in Town would be a small price to pay to save her from the indignities of her current position.

Three pairs of eyes were fixed on the ethereal vision descending the stairs at Priddleton Hall. Adorned in a simple gown of white gauze worn over a maiden-blush slip, Charlotte seemed to float down the steps. The delicate pink of the roses woven both into her dress and her hair was echoed in her softly blushing cheeks.

"Exquisite," said Lady Carstairs, a catch in her voice.

"Perfect," murmured Sarah.

"You beauty!" Sir Horace burst out. "You dashed beauty!"

Charlotte looked rather self-conscious. Her glance took in Sir Horace's pristine silk stockings, the rigid perfection of his linen, and the dark green tailcoat that almost exactly matched his eyes.

"You look rather beautiful yourself, sir"

Sir Horace looked horrified. "No, no, Miss

Fletcher. Can't go about saying a man is beautiful! Not at all the thing!"

Charlotte's colour deepened. "What I meant to say is that your clothing is beautiful. You look very dashing, sir, I assure you."

Sir Horace lowered his raised brows. "Oh! I see. Well that's all right then. Very kind of you to say so."

The assembly rooms at Weymouth were, in the summer season at least, very well attended. It was fortunate then, that they were so spacious they could hold as many as a hundred couples for dancing. Fortunately, it was not quite so crowded as that, for it would have been insufferably hot. Even though he was much occupied, Mr Rodber, the master of ceremonies, made time to welcome them. Whilst he was in conversation with Lady Carstairs, Sarah turned to Charlotte, noting that she had lost some of her sparkle.

"Feeling a little nervous, my dear?"

"Yes," Charlotte admitted, "just a little. It is a pity my cousin and Uncle Oliver are not here. Sir Horace is the only gentleman I know, and I cannot dance with him all evening."

"No, you must not stand up with him more than twice. But you need not feel any anxiety, Charlotte; there are very strict rules governing the behaviour of everyone present, and I do not envisage that you will encounter anything but the utmost politeness from any of the gentlemen here."

"And if you do, Miss Fletcher," Sir Horace said, "you just let me know and I'll know how to deal with them."

"Thank you," she said, looking a little reassured.

Lady Carstairs came up to them. "You need not worry about a thing, Charlotte. I have asked Mr Rodber to ensure that he only introduces you to the most unexceptionable of partners. But I must warn you, that no matter how respectable your partner, you must not dance the waltz. "

"I could not if I wished to," Charlotte said. "Miss Wolfraston did not approve of it and so I have not learnt it."

Lady Carstairs frowned. "How very short-sighted of her. We will have to rectify that before we go to Town. Once you are established there, and have gained the approval of the necessary people, it will be quite acceptable for you to waltz. I would not wish you to suffer the mortification of having to stand at the edge of a ballroom whilst you watch other young ladies being twirled about the floor."

Something in her tone made Sarah suspect that she spoke from painful experience.

"You, Miss Hayes, must certainly waltz if you are given the opportunity." Her eyes rested for a moment on her Grecian round robe of pale green crepe that clung to her delicate curves. "And I am sure you will be, for you look quite ravishing this evening. I'm sure that once Charlotte observes the dance performed correctly, she will have every wish to learn it."

As the couples began to join the first set, the master of ceremonies approached Sarah.

"May I introduce Mr Langton as a suitable partner, ma'am?"

Sarah nodded at the bashful young gentleman and placed her fingers lightly on his arm. They followed Charlotte and Sir Horace onto the floor. She smiled as she heard Charlotte say, "Now, Sir Horace, just remember to listen to the music and all will be well."

And indeed it was. As her partner seemed to have very little to say for himself, Sarah had every opportunity to observe their progress. Sir Horace acquitted himself very well indeed, and at the end of half an hour, again thanked Charlotte profusely for her efforts.

"I think I might just sit the next one out,

though," he said. "Don't want to push my luck too far."

Charlotte wagged a finger at him. "Luck has nothing to do with it. If I am brave enough to stand up with a stranger, then you must surely be."

Mr Rodber just then introduced a gentleman to Charlotte and glanced at Sarah. When she shook her head slightly, he bore Sir Horace off.

Sarah made her way to the row of seats set at the back of the room. She saw that Lady Carstairs was in conversation with another lady. As she drew closer, she saw that it was Lady Turnbull. She frowned and hesitated, but it was too late; Lady Carstairs' eagle eyes were already upon her.

"Why are you not dancing, child?" she said sharply.

"Because, ma'am, I am not a child, but a companion. You can hardly expect me to keep an eye on Charlotte if I am engaged for every dance."

"Nonsense," she said gruffly. "I will undertake that task for this evening."

Sarah turned to Lady Turnbull, noting that the dark shadows were gone and a gentle glow had softened her plain face. "I see your health has continued to improve, ma'am. You look to be in fine form."

"Thank you, Miss Hayes. I am indeed. I have discovered that I am not ill at all, but am expecting a happy event."

Sarah smiled. "Congratulations, ma'am."

Lady Turnbull waved her fan. "I wonder if that is why I am finding it so terrible stuffy in here?"

"I told you not to go racketing about," said her rather poker-faced companion, who sat upon her other side.

"You did indeed, Miss Lavenham," she said in gentle, but firm tones. "But as I am not dancing, I do not think it could be said that I am racketing about precisely."

Miss Lavenham's thin lips puckered in disapproval. Sarah could quite see why Lady Turnbull had wished to attend the ball; she was no doubt in sore need of some congenial company.

"I shall go and procure you a glass of lemonade, ma'am," she said.

Lady Turnbull smiled gratefully at her. "Oh, how very kind you are. That would be the very thing."

She was making her way towards the supper room when she felt a hand steal around her arm.

She glanced up quickly, her eyes widening as they looked into those of Lord Turnbull.

"Unhand me, sir," she said coldly.

"In a moment," he murmured. "Now come along. You do not wish to make a scene, I am sure."

"If there is to be a scene, sir, it will not be of my making."

He smiled down at her in the way she had used to find fascinating.

"I am glad to hear it."

"I am just going to fetch a glass of lemonade for your *wife*," she hissed.

"How very thoughtful of you," he said urbanely. "I can speak with you in the supper room as well as anywhere else. There will be no one about at this early hour."

If this was not quite true, only a few waiters were there, preparing trays of lemonade to refresh the guests between dances.

"Lord Turnbull—"

"You used to call me Robert," he said softly.

"Lord Turnbull," she continued. "Think of my reputation. It would not do if I were to be discovered alone with you."

"Yes, a companion or teacher, cannot afford to sully their fair name." His eyes travelled over her slowly and she felt her colour heighten. "You do not look like any companion I have ever met. It is a pity we are not completely alone."

Her eyes flashed. "I think I made my feelings clear on the last occasion I was unfortunate enough to cross your path," she snapped.

"You did rather," he said wryly. "Took days for that bump to go down."

"Good. Now please, let me take that glass of lemonade to your wife. Her delicate condition is making her feel a little heated."

"Sarah," he said gently. "I know I have caused you much pain. Your anger towards me is completely warranted, and it is better than indifference, at least. But just hear me out, will you?"

She was a little thrown by this change of tactic. She eyed him warily.

"If you still harbour any sort of affection toward me, Lord Turnbull, you would let me go. I do not understand what you can hope to achieve by talking to me."

"Then let me explain," he said. "I discovered at the inn where you had come from and where you were headed. Or at least my groom did. And from there it took only a few enquiries to discover your history. The thought that any action of mine should have been the cause of such a bright, beautiful creature being forced to live such a dull, humdrum life, was torture to me. I do not know how you have survived such an ordeal. I want you to know, that if there had been any way I could have afforded to cherish and protect you, I would have done so."

"I wish you had been as frank with me then, as you are now," Sarah said with some difficulty.

"Yes, perhaps I should have been," he admitted. "But it was not only your hopes and dreams that lay shattered, my dear."

"Well, now you have explained and I must get back—"

"The thing is, Sarah. I *can* now afford to cherish and protect you," he murmured.

Sarah was not sure she could have heard him correctly.

"The life you are leading must be like a living death to you. Would it not be better to live a life of luxury under my protection?"

Her hands curled into fists as indignation swept through her. But even as her lips parted to wound him with the only weapon at her disposal – her words – a dark figure appeared behind him. Lord Seymore tapped Lord Turnbull lightly on the shoulder, and as he turned, delivered a neatly executed punch. Lord Turnbull was sent sprawling on the floor, his nose bleeding profusely. One of the waiters came hurrying up.

"That was as flush a hit as I've ever been privileged to see, sir," he said. "But we don't allow no fighting in the assembly rooms."

Lord Seymore smiled at him. "I am glad to hear it, young fellow. But I don't think one punch qualifies, do you?"

The boy grinned. "No, that it don't, sir."

He turned to Sarah. "Do you have a handkerchief about you, ma'am?"

"Yes, of course," she said, retrieving one from her reticule.

He threw it on top of the prone man. "Better mop yourself up before you get blood all over your cravat and have to explain yourself to your wife."

Lord Turnbull sat up and pressed it to his nose. "Should have known someone would be there before me. It was not gentlemanly of you to take me unawares, Seymore."

"Perhaps not," he acknowledged. "But then I was not dealing with a gentleman." He offered his arm to Sarah. "I think we are finished here, Miss Hayes."

"Almost," she said. "I came to procure a glass of lemonade for Lady Turnbull."

The waiter presented her with one and she accepted Lord Seymore's arm.

"Thank you, sir," she said. "I would very

much have liked to do that myself. It would have given me great satisfaction."

Lord Seymore smiled down at her. "No doubt. But you would have been far more likely to have given yourself a broken hand."

"Yes, I am sure you are right. At least he might finally have got the message now."

Lord Seymore frowned. "Finally? You have met him before?"

She gave him a brief sketch of their former meeting, her eyes kindling with pleasure as she described hitting him over the head with the water jug.

Lord Seymore's glower turned to a look of amusement.

"How very resourceful you are."

"Oh, you here at last, Seymore," Lady Carstairs said as they approached.

"As you see, ma'am."

"Well better late than never, I suppose."

"I came as swiftly as I could, I assure you, ma'am."

Sarah handed the lemonade to Lady Turnbull, not quite able to meet her eyes.

"Justin! You are here. I am so glad. Now I can dance the next set with you," Charlotte said, just then coming up on the arm of Sir Horace.

Sarah saw a warm smile curve his lips as he took his ward's hands.

"You look radiant, my dear. I would be honoured to dance with you." He turned to Sir Horace. "Enjoying yourself?"

"Never would have believed it possible, but I am. Even managed to talk to my partner a little during the last dance, and what's more, she didn't look at me as if I was queer as Dick's hatband!"

"A triumph indeed," he laughed.

Sir Horace's gaze dropped to the hint of waistcoat that could be seen by the lapels of Lord Seymore's blue coat. "I say, that's a dashed fine waistcoat, Seymore. The pink flowers are exquisite, the only thing is, not sure it's quite the thing for a ball."

"Perhaps not," he conceded. "But I have to let my valet have his way occasionally, old fellow, or he might leave me for a more adventurous gentleman."

Sir Horace had no fault to find with this logic. Lord Seymore was pleased, however, that Mr Rodber chose that moment to announce the next dance. It was a waltz.

"I shall have to sit this one out," Charlotte said, a little regretfully.

"Never mind. I shall keep you company," Sir Horace assured her.

"I would not wish to keep you from it, if you think you would enjoy it," Charlotte said, with a shy smile.

"You may rest easy on that head, Miss Fletcher," he assured her. "If you ain't dancing it with me, I wouldn't enjoy it, simple as that."

"Well go on, Seymore," Lady Carstairs said peremptorily, "take Miss Hayes onto the floor and show Charlotte how it is done."

For some reason, Sarah felt a blush steal into her cheeks, but she laid her hand on his and allowed herself to be led onto the floor. As his arm curled around her waist, she found herself rather tongue-tied. Her eyes remained firmly fixed on the top button of his coat.

After a few moments, he said pensively, "Have I quite sunk myself in your estimation, ma'am?"

She glanced up surprised. "How can you say so? I stand very much in your debt, sir."

"You have relieved my mind, ma'am. But when you could not take your eyes from my waistcoat, I feared the worst."

"I must admit that it is something I would expect Sir Horace to wear, rather than you."

Lord Seymore seemed much struck by this.

"Thank you, Miss Hayes, you have provided the solution to a thorny problem. I shall give it to him as a gift."

"But what would your poor valet, say?"

"He will be quite mortified that he has mislaid it, of course," he acknowledged. "But I shall be very understanding, you may be sure."

CHAPTER 14

Mr Fancot returned to Priddleton Hall the day after the ball. Lady Carstairs, who had been keeping an eye out for her husband's return, was both surprised and disappointed to see him trot up to the house on a hired hack, alone. She intercepted him as he entered the house.

"Where is Carstairs?" she said, without preamble. "Do not tell me he is ill?"

Mr Fancot looked a little taken aback by this greeting. "No, ma'am. Not as far as I am aware. He spent only one night at Filton. He recalled that he had friends in the area and decided to pay them a visit."

"What friends?" she demanded.

"I am not sure, ma'am. He did not say, or if he did, I have forgotten."

"Really!" she said, clearly put out. "I do not suppose he thought I would be interested in this change to his plans as he has sent me no word. How long does he intend to stay with these friends?"

"Only one night, ma'am. There was no point in him writing as he should be back sometime today."

Lady Carstairs looked a little mollified. "Oh, I see. That puts quite a different complexion on the matter."

"How is my mother?" Mr Fancot asked, a little warily.

"That I cannot tell you," Lady Carstairs said, a little frostily. "I have twice been to visit Mrs Fancot, but have been informed on both occasions that she was not at home to visitors."

Mr Fancot frowned. "Please, do not take any offence, ma'am. My mother is sometimes prone to fits of dejection, and at these times she will see no one, not even myself."

"I shall make her a tincture from the flowers of St John's wort, it is meant to be quite effective at alleviating melancholy."

"Thank you, ma'am. I will mention it to her

when I visit her later," Mr Fancot said, bowing, before hurrying up the stairs.

Sarah found Lady Carstairs standing in the hall, her thoughts far away, not many moments later.

"Ma'am?" she said gently.

Lady Carstairs started. "Miss Hayes." She glanced at Sarah's riding habit. "You're very late for your ride this morning."

"Very," she acknowledged. "I am no longer used to such late nights and overslept this morning. Is all well? I could not help but notice that you looked a little worried just now."

"Did I?"

"Yes," Sarah said gently. "I am a very good listener."

When Lady Carstairs looked a little uncertain, Sarah glanced at the footman who stood statue-like, near the stairs. "Come, let us go somewhere a little more private." She looked again at the footman. "Make sure we are not disturbed will you, James?"

He remained rigidly upright, only his eyes swivelling in her direction. "Yes, ma'am."

"Really, Miss Hayes," Lady Carstairs protested, as she found herself gently but firmly propelled across the hall, "there is really nothing wrong with me."

"I do not mean to be rude, but that is a plumper if ever I heard one," Sarah said, guiding her into the drawing room and shutting the door softly behind them. "I am very discreet, I assure you."

"You will think me mad," Lady Carstairs said, eyeing her doubtfully. "I have thought so myself several times over the last few days."

Sarah smiled. "Eccentric, perhaps, but never mad, ma'am."

"I hope you will still think so in a very few minutes, Miss Hayes," Lady Carstairs said, sitting down.

Sarah took the seat opposite her, folded her hands on her lap, and looked at her expectantly.

"The thing is, Miss Hayes, I have recently been struck by thoughts that are as outrageous as they are preposterous. It is not like me at all."

Lady Carstairs began to fiddle with the fringe of her shawl as if not quite certain of how to proceed.

"I take it that this has something to do with Lord Carstairs?" she prompted her.

Lady Carstairs sighed, low and long. "You are very perceptive, my dear."

Sarah smiled. "I could not help but notice that you did not appear at all pleased that he was visiting Mrs Fancot."

"I was not," she said shortly. "There is something about her that I cannot quite like, although I cannot put my finger upon what it is. And then…" she paused, and then said, a little awkwardly, "she is still a very attractive woman."

"I thought that might be it," Sarah said gently. "Although I do not think you need worry on that account."

"You don't?"

"No. I would need to be blind not to notice Lord Carstairs' very real affection and admiration for you."

An unusually soft smile curved Lady Carstairs' lips. "Yes. I am very fortunate in that regard." The smiled faded. "It seemed a little odd, however, that he should take upon himself the duty of visiting her."

"Perhaps he thought you had enough to do with a house full of guests."

"Perhaps," she conceded. "But I'm afraid that my initial reservations about him doing so were supplanted by others that were far more ridiculous."

Sarah raised an enquiring brow.

"It occurred to me that Carstairs only began to feel ill after his visits to Mrs Fancot began."

Sarah made a noise somewhere between a laugh and a gasp. "But, ma'am, you cannot mean… no, surely you cannot. I was under the impression that he already has a condition that sometimes causes him to be ill."

Lady Carstairs eyes sharpened. "As I have not informed anyone of that myself, Miss Hayes, I would be very interested to know how it comes about that you know of it."

Sarah coloured. "Lord Seymore and I met him just after he had returned from a visit to Mrs Fancot. He was a little pale and complained of palpitations. He said it was his old complaint."

"I cannot help but wonder why you did not see fit to inform me of this," she said, a little coldly.

"I was not quite comfortable keeping it from you, I assure you. But Lord Carstairs did not wish to worry you. He did promise, however, that if he should continue to feel unwell, he would send for the doctor and inform you of the circumstance."

"I see," she said. "Well, if you do not already think me stark raving mad, you will when I tell you that although his heart condition may well explain his sudden decline in health, I could not rid myself of the thought that both Mrs Fancot and her son would have much to gain if something happened to my lord. He has suffered none of his symptoms for some months now, after all. And I have ensured, to the best of my ability, that he has not overtaxed himself since our return."

"If you do not mind me saying so, ma'am, I fear your concern has begun to chafe him a little. He said something about things being left too long inactive, withering and dying. He was referring to the phaeton but I did wonder if he might not also so be referring to himself."

"You are right," Lady Carstairs said a little glumly. "I have noticed his irritation myself. It is why I made no demur when he decided to go to Filton. But now Mr Fancot has come back alone. Apparently, Carstairs has gone to visit friends and will be back later today."

Sarah chuckled. "Lady Carstairs, you are a sensible woman. You cannot believe that he has done away with Lord Carstairs."

"No, I don't suppose I do. I told you my thoughts were outrageous and preposterous, did I not?" A relieved smile twisted her lips. "Thank you, Miss Hayes. When one keeps ones worries to oneself, they can grow out of all proportion. Go and take your ride. I expect Lord Seymore is waiting for you."

"I shall," Sarah said, rising to her feet. "And

I would not be at all surprised if by the time we return, Lord Carstairs has arrived."

As she made her way back through the great hall, she saw Charlotte and Sir Horace. They both carried sketchbooks and Sir Horace had a blanket thrown over one shoulder.

"We are going to draw down by the river," Charlotte said. "I hope to see the kingfishers for myself."

"Very well," Sarah said. "But as you will not be able to hold your parasol and draw at the same time, might I suggest that you sit on the far bank under the trees? It is very hot again today."

"Don't you worry, Miss Hayes," Sir Horace said. "I will take every care of Miss Fletcher, you may be sure."

"I do not doubt it," she said smiling. "I do not suppose I should let you go off together un-chaperoned, but as I am about to go riding with Lord Seymore, that would be the pot calling the kettle black."

Lord Seymore paced up and down, completely oblivious of the knowing looks the stable hands shared behind his back. Miss Hayes had agreed at breakfast to meet him at eleven o'clock, and it was already nearly half past the hour. Perhaps she had changed her mind. His glance strayed towards the entrance of the yard, as it had several times before, but dropped back to the cobbles when he saw she was not there. He hoped that she had not. The events of the night before had made his feelings towards her as clear as glass.

He was rarely driven to anger, but only Miss Hayes' presence had prevented him from pummelling Lord Turnbull to a pulp last evening. For her sake, he had, with some effort, managed to preserve a calm demeanour, but he had put all his disgust into the one blow he had allowed himself. When she had described their previous encounter he had regretted his forbearance, but only for an instant. The undisguised relish with which she had described hitting Turnbull over the head with a jug had triggered their shared sense of the ridiculous. He would very much like to claim the right to protect her from any and all indignities that her present position might afford her.

He too, had slept late this morning, as he had spent hours after he had fallen into bed following Lucy's advice and practicing his address. He had not managed to achieve anything he was remotely satisfied with, however.

"I am sorry if I have kept you waiting, Lord Seymore, but I ran into Lady Carstairs and we fell to talking."

His head snapped up, a wide smile dawning as he saw the elegant figure walking towards him.

"I expect she was twitching about Mr Fancot coming back without Lord Carstairs."

"Exactly so," she said.

Two stable boys promptly brought out the horses that had been ready for some time. He threw her up into the saddle before swiftly mounting his own steed.

"Where to today?"

"If you have no objection, we will just go for a gallop through the park and then circle back to the river. Charlotte has gone there with Sir Horace to draw, and I cannot help but feel that I ought to at least keep a cursory eye on her."

Lord Seymore grinned, his eyes crinkling. "You need have no fears on that head, Miss Hayes. As her guardian, I have none at all. Sir Horace would never do anything in the least improper or that he would consider *not the thing*."

"I know it," she said. "Otherwise I would have forgone my ride and accompanied them."

Once they had enjoyed a good gallop, they slowed their horses to a walk and turned in the general direction of the river, content now to dawdle. Their eyes met and they shared a companionable smile.

"I hope your business at Winbourne was concluded successfully?"

"It was," Lord Seymore confirmed, a glimmer of amusement in his eyes.

He described his encounter with the salt officer and was pleased when she saw the absurdity of it.

"Is smuggling so very rife in Lymington?"

"It is rumoured that a network of tunnels run under the town, but as the customs officers have never discovered any, I find that unlikely in the extreme. It wouldn't surprise me if there are one or two though."

"You do not seem unduly worried by this."

He shrugged fatalistically. "Whilst taxes remain so high, it is inevitable."

She shook her head and said on a sigh, "And I thought you such a respectable gentleman. How easily one is deceived."

"I am," he laughed. "But I would much prefer to expend my energies on things that concern me more nearly."

"Such as?"

"Making sure my tenants are content and my estate runs at a profit."

"Very commendable," she murmured with a rather wistful smile, her eyes losing their focus.

She was, he felt sure, thinking of her father. It had not been his intention to draw a comparison between them, but perhaps it was no bad thing. She would not wish to ally herself to someone who could not offer her a secure future.

Nyx came to a halt and dropped her head to nibble the grass, as if aware that her rider was not paying attention. Sarah smiled wryly at her escort. "Forgive me, I was wool-gathering. Where were we? Oh yes, Winbourne. Although I understand Sir Francis wished to be rid of Mr Fawlty, I am surprised he felt the need to call you home. I do not see that your presence was strictly necessary; he could have gone in your stead. I am pleased that you returned in time for the ball, at all events."

His moment had come he realised. He cleared his throat. "There was another reason as it happens."

"Oh?"

"He wished me to offer for his daughter, Lucy."

Her eyes turned swiftly to his, they clearly showed her surprise and something else he hoped was disappointment.

"And did you?" she said brightly.

"Yes, but—"

He got no further, for a piercing scream disturbed the still air.

"It is Charlotte!" Sarah said.

Lord Seymore nodded and they galloped towards the river. As they had already been moving in that direction, they reached it in under a minute. Mr Fancot was standing in the river up to his knees, his eyes fixed on a point just beyond the bridge. They saw a flash of white and two thrashing arms. Lord Seymore was off his horse in an instant. He sprinted towards the bridge and saw Sir Horace running down the bank in the other direction. He suddenly dived into the water and by the time Lord Seymore reached the spot, he had Charlotte safely to the bank. Her hands were clasped tightly around his neck and she was sobbing uncontrollably.

"How on earth did you let such a thing happen?" Lord Seymore snapped.

When Sir Horace raised his head from Charlotte's, his expression was so tortured that Lord Seymore felt his anger at his friend dissipate.

"I thought I saw a goshawk," he gasped, his chest heaving. "I'd only been gone a few minutes. Lost sight of it amongst the trees and was on my way back when I heard the scream. I don't know how such a thing could have happened."

"My poor child," Sarah cried, just then reaching them. She turned to Lord Seymore. "We must get her back, quickly. She will need to be dried and warmed urgently if she is not to become ill."

Sir Horace stood with her still in his arms.

"Give her to me," said Lord Seymore.

But Charlotte clung even closer to Sir Horace and he shook his head.

"I will carry her as far as your horse, Seymore."

He had just passed her up to him when Mr Fancot approached them.

"Will she be all right?" he said, his voice sombre.

"Let us hope so," Sarah said, with some asperity. "But if she is, it will be no thanks to you, sir, when you just stood there watching her float away down the river!"

Charlotte's sobbing had lessened considerably and she managed to gasp, "H-he, p-pushed me in!"

As Lord Seymore and Sarah turned amazed gazes on the man, Sir Horace stepped forwards and dealt him a perfectly executed uppercut. He went down like a stone. Sir Horace stood over him, his fists clenched.

"Get up, man! Get up!" he growled. "I haven't finished with you yet!"

"He is out cold," Lord Seymore said flatly. "I will send Greeves down with a cart to take him back. Do not let him out of your sight; he will have some questions to answer presently. We must get Charlotte back."

"Yes, you must," said Sir Horace, testily. "I don't know why you're still here. Be off with you!"

CHAPTER 15

S arah and Lady Carstairs briskly rubbed
Charlotte down whilst Mrs Baines herself
made up the fire in her bedchamber. By
the time she was wrapped up in both a nightshift
and a dressing gown, and bundled into bed,
some colour had returned to her cheeks.

"There, my dear," Sarah said, brushing a
tendril of hair away from her forehead. "You
look much better already."

Charlotte smiled wanly. "Yes, I do not feel
unwell. It was only the shock."

"I shall send you a sustaining broth, Miss
Fletcher," Mrs Baines said solicitously.

Lady Carstairs looked upon her with an unusually benevolent eye. "Thank you, Mrs Baines.
You always know just what is required."

"I am pleased you think so, ma'am."

As she left the room, Lord Carstairs entered it, a deep frown furrowing his brow.

"Carstairs!" his good lady cried. "You are back. Thank heavens!"

She would have said more but he kissed her hand and shook his head slightly. "Would you mind leaving me to have a word with Charlotte, alone, for a moment, my dear? Await me in the library. I should not be long."

"She needs to rest—"

"I do not mind," Charlotte said quietly. "I am pleased to see you, Uncle Oliver."

He went over to the bed and took the hand that lay on the coverlet between both his own. "And I, you, my child."

Sarah and Lady Carstairs exchanged a look and then went out onto the landing. The arrival of her lord, seemed to have robbed Lady Carstairs of her usual composure, for she suddenly blinked rapidly and gave a strangled sob. Sarah handed her a handkerchief and she wiped her eyes and blew her nose.

"Thank you, my dear," she said, a little shakily. "In all my wildest imaginings, I did not foresee such an event as this. I do not pretend to understand it. What could have driven Mr Fancot to do such a thing?"

"I do not know, ma'am," Sarah said quietly. "He was, at first, a little jealous of Sir Horace's friendship with Charlotte, but I thought all that had changed once he met Miss Truboot. But even if it had not, he would have to be quite, quite mad to do such a thing. And even if he was in a jealous rage, it is surely Sir Horace who would suffer the consequences and not Charlotte. No, that cannot be it. Perhaps there is an innocent explanation, after all."

"Hrmf! I would like to know how you accidentally push someone into the river!"

They found Lord Seymore in the library.

"How is she?" he asked, rising swiftly from his chair.

"She is much improved," Sarah assured him.

His shoulders sagged in relief. "Thank God!"

"And Sir Horace," she said softly.

"Indeed," said Lady Carstairs. "Although I am not at all pleased that he left her alone, even for a short time, I am delighted he knocked Mr Fancot down. Never knew he had it in him!"

"What a bloodthirsty set of females you are," Lord Seymore said dryly.

"Where *is* Sir Horace?" Sarah asked.

"He waited only to change out of his wet things before setting up camp outside Mr Fancot's door. He has taken it upon himself to be his jailor. If he tries to bolt, he will regret it."

"I wish he had tried it," Sir Horace said, coming into the room. "Lord Carstairs has relieved me of duty. He sent me down here whilst he has a word with him."

"You've left him on his own with Mr Fancot?" Lady Carstairs said, incredulously.

"Didn't like it, ma'am, I assure you. But he insisted. Mind you, I made sure your footman took my place first. Told him to wait there in case Lord Carstairs decided to send for a doctor."

"Well, that is something, I suppose," she conceded.

Silence fell upon the room as each of the occupants became lost in their own thoughts. It was half an hour before Lord Carstairs joined them. He was accompanied by Mr Fancot. He looked rather pale and was a little unsteady on his feet. A dull red colour suffused his cheeks, however, as he felt the accusatory stares of the rest of the party upon him.

"Sit down, Charles, before you fall down," Lord Carstairs said gently.

He sank gratefully into a convenient armchair, his gaze rooted to the floor.

"I would ask you all to be seated."

A change had come over Lord Carstairs. There was a ring of authority in his tone. It was as if he had put off the mantle of genial host, and taken on the one he had worn for many years as a successful judge.

When everyone had complied with his suggestion, he said, "I do not wish for any interruptions over the next few minutes. None at all." His eyes rested on his wife for a moment, before sweeping over the other occupants of the room. "No doubt you will have many questions, but they must wait until I am ready to answer them. I wish to brush through the interview I am about to conduct as quickly and efficiently as possible. If that is not acceptable to any of you, I must ask you to leave. Do I make myself clear?"

"Very well, Carstairs," his wife said, a bemused but respectful look in her eyes.

"I must also insist that nothing you hear today, goes beyond this room. If you cannot guarantee your silence, I must also ask you to leave."

When no one complied with this command, he nodded briefly and began.

"Charles, did you push Miss Fletcher in the river?"

"No."

"Likely story—" Sir Horace began, but Lord Carstairs' steely look silenced him.

"Can you please explain how you came to be at the river, Charles?"

Mr Fancot leant his head back against the chair, and closed his eyes. "I was walking through the wood, on the way to visit my mother. I had decided that it was time to make my peace with her. I had just reached the track that leads to the dower house when I heard a scream. I ran down to the river and saw Miss Fletcher submerged in the water. I waded in to try and help her." He paused and grimaced. "I will never forget the expression of horror on her face when she resurfaced. I tried to catch hold of her, but the current is very strong there and it swept her away from me." His voice broke on the words, his distress clear.

"Why did you not go in after her?" Lord Carstairs said gently.

"Because I cannot swim. The river is very deep at that point. Even if I had managed to reach her, I would have been more likely to have drowned us both rather than save her. It all happened so fast. I was about to run along the bank in the hope that she would stay afloat until the river becomes shallower, but Miss Hayes and Lord Seymore arrived before I could do so."

Lord Carstairs turned to Lord Seymore. "Did you hear Miss Fletcher scream, sir?"

"Yes," he confirmed.

"How long after you heard the scream, did you arrive at the riverbank?"

"It cannot have been more than a minute."

"And what did you see when you arrived?"

"Mr Fancot standing in the water, watching Charlotte."

"Very good. I think you will agree that there are no discrepancies in either of your stories thus far?"

"Except for the fact that Charlotte claimed he had pushed her," Lord Seymore said, putting a restraining hand on Sir Horace when he moved as if to jump up.

When he had sunk back into his chair, Lord Carstairs continued.

"Miss Fletcher never saw who pushed her in. She only saw Mr Fancot climbing down the bank, and assumed it was him."

"But there was no one else there, dash it!" protested Sir Horace, unable to remain silent any longer.

"Not at that moment, no. But there must have been someone else there only moments before, as I am certain Charles speaks the truth."

He let that sink in for a moment before

turning again to that gentleman. "How long did it take you to arrive at the riverbank after you heard the scream, Charles?"

"Perhaps thirty seconds," he said. "She had fallen in a little way further up the river and I tried to grab her as she swept past me."

Lord Carstairs nodded. He looked at the assembled company. "Charlotte has confirmed that she wandered further along the bank as she saw a flash of turquoise and thought it must be the kingfisher she was so keen to see. As the trees reach almost to the edge of the bank at that point, I would suggest that it would be very easy for someone to quickly conceal themselves there. Would you agree Charles?"

"Yes," he said, sitting forwards and dropping his head into his hands.

"And did you see or hear anything that might have suggested that someone was there?"

A low moan escaped him. "I heard the crack of twigs breaking, as if someone were running through the undergrowth, just as Lord Seymore and Miss Hayes arrived."

"Very convenient," Sir Horace muttered.

Lord Carstairs sent him a quelling glance.

"And did you look to see who it might be?"

"Yes," Mr Fancot said heavily. "I saw the flash of a black gown."

Lady Carstairs gasped. "So it was Mrs Fancot that pushed Charlotte in the river. I knew——"

Lord Carstairs put up his hand and she was silenced.

"Although I hate to cause you any further pain or embarrassment, Charles, I think I really must ask you to enlighten the present company as to the cause of your argument with your mother."

He sighed and ran a hand through his hair, his eyes still fixed upon the carpet. "Although mother refuses to come here or go anywhere for that matter, she is always hungry for information. She demands an account of everyone I meet, and insists I repeat whole conversations to her. It is why I returned to the hall; I could stand it no longer. Especially as, as…" He trailed off and took a deep breath.

"Did you perhaps overhear the conversation I had with Lord Seymore the day he arrived?" Lord Carstairs interjected.

Mr Fancot nodded. "Yes. I told her you were going to create a trust for Miss Fletcher. I did not see the harm. Only she became rather obsessed by the information. She insisted I try to fix my interest with her. That is why she came to dinner the next evening; she wished to judge for herself how things stood. She said you shouldn't be giving away money that was rightfully mine. I told her I liked Miss Fletcher very well, but that considerations such as that would not weigh with me. And I meant it, sir," he said, raising his head at last. "I am heir to this estate only by chance. I am far more comfortable as a steward than I ever would be as an earl."

Lord Carstairs went over to Mr Fancot and dropped a hand on his shoulder. "I believe you, Charles. You have said enough for now, I believe, and I would save you any further awkwardness. Go back to your room and rest."

As soon as the door shut behind him, Lord Carstairs turned to his wife. "You were saying, my dear?"

"Only that I knew there was something, apart from what we spoke of before you left, that I did not like about the woman. You will call me foolish, but I had almost persuaded myself that she was poisoning you!"

Lord Carstairs looked grave. "I have always said you were a remarkable woman."

The discovery that she was not mad after all, clearly offered Lady Carstairs little comfort. She raised a slightly unsteady hand to her cheek and murmured, "Oh, this is terrible!"

Lord Carstairs sank into the chair Mr Fancot had just vacated. "It is indeed."

"It was the tart!" she suddenly exclaimed, sitting bolt upright. "She has a cherry laurel hedge in her garden! I noticed it when I went to call. The leaves, once distilled, smell of almonds! It is often used to flavour creams and puddings but only a very dilute, small amount must be used or it is poisonous! Oh, I have been such a fool! I should have realised earlier."

"That you realised at all, is a mark of your intelligence, my dear."

"I saw Mrs Fancot clipping leaves from a hedge in her garden when I drove your phaeton, sir," Sarah said quietly. "Are you certain it was not a mistake? There is a vast difference between perhaps yielding to the impulse of the moment, and plotting a cold blooded murder!"

"I wish I could think it," he said softly. "I think she hoped to make it look like a natural event. The first doses were small enough to only make me ill. But the tart she gave me to take to Filton would have proved fatal, had I eaten it."

"How do you know that, Carstairs? Do not tell me someone else has suffered that fate?"

"No, not *someone*. I did not know then what I meant to do. I kept the tart in my room, unsure if I would need it as evidence. But I am afraid I had not considered the mice. Apparently there is quite an infestation at Filton. They made a feast of it and I found five of them dead in the morning."

Lady Carstairs blanched. "Are you sure Mr Fancot did not know of this? How could Mrs Fancot have known that he would not partake of a slice?"

He gave her a rather grim smile. "You are not as observant as I had thought, my dear. Have you not noticed that Charles never touches the desert course at dinner?"

"No, I have not," she admitted. "I can't say I pay any particular attention to what he eats." A look of indignation suddenly crossed her face. "Carstairs! Knowing that woman was a black-hearted murderer, you sent me to visit her in your absence! How could you?"

"Ah, but I had taken steps to ensure you were not admitted to the house, my dear. Mrs Biddy, the housekeeper there, is an old retainer of the family. I asked her to tell you Mrs Fancot was not at home to visitors if you went calling. She was also told to keep a very close eye on her movements. But I am afraid she evaded her today."

"Why could you not have shared your suspicions?" Lady Carstairs said, clearly a little hurt.

He sighed. "Because all was still only conjecture and the idea seemed fabulous. I only knew then that I felt much better after I had purged myself after eating the second helping of her tart, and not at all ill on the day I threw it away. I was, however, somewhat disturbed by our little talks. She spoke to me of years of misery at the hands of her husband and how jealous he was if another man so much as looked at her. How he used to lock her up in her room and even keep her son away from her at times."

"On the day she and her son argued, she told me that Mr Fancot had a temper like his father," Sarah said quietly. "I remember how surprised I was, for Mr Fancot is, in general, a very moderate gentleman."

"Precisely. And he has always spoken very fondly of his father, who came here not long before I went to India. I did not know him well, but my recollections were of a very gentle man." He glanced at his wife. "And then there was the business you brought to me the night before we left."

"My lord," Lady Carstairs said a little uneasily. "Do you really think we should discuss this in front of our guests."

A laugh shook her lord. "You always did have an odd quirk of prudery in your character, my dear. You do not mind them hearing all the rest, yet you baulk at an indiscretion. Tell them what Lady Crossington whispered in your ear on the evening of that dreadful dinner."

"Is it true?" she asked.

"Yes, it is," he confirmed.

"Very well. Lady Crossington has lived in these parts for many years. She said that there had been a whisper that Mrs Fancot was with child before she was wed, and that Mr Fancot married her to save her from disgrace. That is why they moved parish not long afterwards."

"That won't fadge," Sir Horace said confidently. "He has the nose. Was looking at the portraits upstairs whilst I sat outside Fancot's room, and dashed if all the Fancot's don't have it, including you, sir. Very distinct, hooked like a bird of prey."

Lord Seymore's eyes strayed to the lectern that was sculpted in the shape of an eagle. His brows rose. A green, leather box sat upon the stand. "You have found the book, sir."

"I have indeed." Lord Carstairs said softly. "Or rather Mrs Biddy did at my instigation. But I already knew what Mrs Fancot was at pains to hide from me and her son. Mr Fancot is more closely related to me than I had imagined, you see. He is my brother's son."

"So it was the earl who she meant when she said his father had a temper."

"Yes, Miss Hayes. I rather think that Mrs Fancot, or Miss Lindon, as she was then, had set her sights on becoming a countess. She was very beautiful remember, and quite naïve it seems. I spent some time with Mrs Rawlins, the house-keeper at the parsonage at Filton. Very illumi-nating I found it too. It is a very quiet, out of the way place, and did not suit Mrs Fancot at all. She became increasingly disgruntled over the years and frequently oscillated between fits of dejection and uncontrollable rages. The doctor sedated her at these times, and it fell to Mrs Rawlins to watch over her. She told me enough of what she called her 'wild ravings', to confirm all my suspicions. I feel very sorry for her."

"That is coming it a little too strong, Carstairs," his good lady protested.

"Do you think so, my dear?" he said mildly. "My brother took advantage of her, got her with child, and then abandoned her. Her employer would have certainly thrown her out and she would have been left on the parish if my cousin had not stepped into the breech. He adored her, according to Mrs Rawlins. She said it grieved him greatly that he could not make her happy.

But there was little chance of that, her temper has been uneven since she was a child."

"And how do you know that, Carstairs?"

"The marriage record, my dear. I checked it before I left. It stated Mrs Fancot's maiden name and her parish of birth. I visited her parents yesterday."

"You have been busy, sir," Lord Seymore said with a faint smile.

"I wanted to have all the facts at my disposal before I came to a decision as to what to do next," he said pensively.

"And what will you do, sir?" Sarah said.

"I shall send her to her parents." He glanced at Lord Seymore. "That is if you do not object, sir? As Miss Fletcher's guardian, I acknowledge that you should have some say in the matter. Mr and Mrs Lindon are very respectable people. They own a large farm in a very remote area. Their daughter began to be subject to mood swings in her teens. She did not enjoy living in such a rural situation. She was sent to live as a companion to a widowed aunt, who had married a merchant and was reasonably well-to-do. But that lady could not put up with her moodiness and sent her back home. Only she did not arrive. She became a companion to a Mrs Cricket, not five miles from here. She met my brother, whether by design or accident is unclear, and the rest you know. Her parents are, of course, much grieved by what has occurred, but they have agreed to take her in. I will provide a suitable woman to watch over her, of course."

Lord Seymore considered his words for a moment. "Your plan seems sound enough, sir. I would not subject Charlotte or your family to an unpleasant investigation, as long as I am assured Mrs Fancot will be no further danger to anyone."

"Now just wait a minute!" Sir Horace said, clearly outraged. "The woman has attempted murder twice, and her only punishment is to be sent to a farm in the country?"

"It will be punishment enough," Lord Carstairs said gently. "Remember, Sir Horace, that she is being sent back to the very place she could not wait to escape from, all her hopes and dreams in tatters. She will be kept sedated when necessary and under strict watch at all times. Once she arrives at the farm, she will never again leave it. It is kinder than sending her to an asylum for the insane, which is surely where she would otherwise end up, but only just."

"But will she go?" Lord Seymore said.

"She already knows her fate," Lord Carstairs

said wearily, "I saw her before I came up to the house."

"Was that wise?" Lord Seymore said.

"Mrs Biddy was present at the interview but the fewer people who know of this, the better. She did fall into an unseemly rage but we managed to restrain her. She is at present locked in her room."

He frowned. "Charles brought her here with the best of intentions. But it only fuelled his mother's resentment." His eyes turned towards the door as a knock fell upon it. "I made it clear we were not to be disturbed. I expect it is Riddle convinced we can no longer survive without some refreshment to sustain us. No matter, a glass of wine would not go amiss. Come!"

But it was not Riddle who came hastily through the door, but a harassed looking lady of middling years, dressed neatly, a cap set upon her grey locks. The keys dangling on her chatelaine marked her position.

"Mrs Biddy!" Lord Carstairs exclaimed, rising to his feet.

This lady cast an anxious look at the rest of the company.

"They know all," Lord Carstairs said quickly. "What has happened?"

"It's Mrs Fancot, sir. I was just going to

check on her when I heard a thud. By the time I opened her door she was in convulsions on the floor, her lips had turned blue, and then she went still." She raised a handkerchief to her lips for a moment. "She's stone dead, sir. A small bottle of cherry laurel water was on the floor beside her."

A stunned silence greeted these words. Lord Carstairs was the first to recover.

"Go back to the dower house, Mrs Biddy. Mr Fancot and I will come to you in a moment and I will send James footman to fetch Doctor Smeathley."

"Oh, the poor woman!" Sarah said. "Can I be of any assistance, sir?"

"Thank you, Miss Hayes. But no. The only thing any of you can do is to keep mum about the business."

He went out of the room but instantly returned and addressed Lord Seymore.

"It has just occurred to me that once Charlotte is made aware of today's events, her spirits, which are already quite low, are likely to sink even further. Might I suggest, sir, that it may be better to remove her from Priddleton for a short while, until this unpleasant business is over?"

"I think it a very sensible suggestion, sir. I

shall take her and Miss Hayes to Winbourne tomorrow."

"Thank you, sir. I think the next few days will prove very difficult for Charles. Indeed, I expect he will hardly feel able to show his face. I think it might be easier for him to bear the weight of the shame he is bound to feel, if only I remain here. I wonder——" Lord Carstairs' weary gaze rested on his wife for a moment.

"Lady Carstairs and Sir Horace are, of course, welcome, sir," Lord Seymore said.

"But, my lord," Lady Carstairs said, "you must not take everything upon yourself. Let me stay and help you."

He came to her and took her hand. "My love, I shall miss you terribly, of course, but I must insist. Charles must be my first concern, and we will brush through this terrible business far more swiftly if I am not distracted by my lovely wife."

"Palaverer!" she said brusquely.

"Having all her friends about her will enable Charlotte to regain her equilibrium far more quickly, I am sure."

"Oh, very well! But promise me you won't overtax yourself, Carstairs."

He dropped a swift kiss on her hand. "I

promise. I shall come and fetch you myself, probably in about a week."

He was gone on the words.

Sarah stood. "I will go to Charlotte, she has been alone long enough."

"I will come with you," Lord Seymore said. "I wish to satisfy myself that she is well."

They found Charlotte fast asleep. Sarah walked quickly to the bed and laid the back of her hand against her forehead. "All is well," she said softly. "There is no fever."

Lord Seymore looked down at her for a long moment. "I only hope she will not suffer any nightmares."

"I shall not leave her side this night," Sarah said. "I shall have a truckle bed set up in here."

He sent her a grateful look. "Thank you. I will see you at dinner then."

"I think I will have something sent up here," she said. "I have no appetite and I would not wish her to awaken and find no one here."

"Very well, ma'am. I must go and inform my valet that he must go ahead and warn my house-keeper of our imminent arrival."

He bowed and left the room. Sarah sat beside the bed and took one of Charlotte's hands. She absently stroked her thumb along the back of it. So much had happened today, and all of it quite horrid. She would be forever grateful to Sir Horace for rescuing Charlotte. She was sure the empty feeling inside her was delayed shock; it could not possibly have anything to do with the revelation Lord Seymore had made just before they had heard Charlotte scream. She was sure it was nothing to her if he were to be married, after all.

CHAPTER 16

Feeling that Charlotte had suffered enough unpleasantness for one day, Sarah waited until the following morning to disclose to her the truth about Mrs Fancot. It was a testament to her gentle nature that she evinced some sympathy for her. What troubled her most was that the lady had taken her own life, and she could not rid herself of the notion that she had, in some part, been responsible for this desperate act. Sarah was very pleased that after an early breakfast, they immediately left for Winbourne. Hopefully, the change of scene would give her thoughts another direction.

They were eight hours upon the road, and each one seemed to crawl by. Charlotte remained very withdrawn throughout the journey, every now and then dissolving into a bout of weeping. Nothing Lady Carstairs or Sarah said consoled her, and their own conversation was stilted as they attempted to avoid, whenever possible, all reference to the recent events that were naturally uppermost in their minds.

Charlotte roused herself a little when, after welcoming Lady Carstairs and Miss Hayes, Mrs Norton turned to her and said warmly, "How glad I am to welcome you back to Winbourne, Miss Fletcher. You have grown into the beautiful young woman you always promised to be."

"Thank you, Mrs Norton," she said softly.

"It is such a shame that you did not come again after your first visit. But I am determined to make you so comfortable that you will not wish to leave this time."

"Do not make us too comfortable, Mrs Norton," Lady Carstairs said dryly, "Or I too, may not wish to leave. This house appears to be very elegantly appointed and I suspect not the suspicion of a draught dare penetrate the windows."

"I should hope not, my lady," the housekeeper said with a small smile. "Lady Seymore, God rest her soul, liked everything just so. It must be ten years now since she passed. It is not to be expected that gentlemen should take so close an interest, but I have always kept things as she would have liked them to be in honour of her memory."

"Very right, too," said Lady Carstairs approvingly. She glanced at two large vases that stood on small tables on either side of the staircase. "It appears you have some delightful blooms at Winbourne."

"Yes, ma'am. I pick them myself. I always think they brighten a room. I have put some in all of your chambers."

"Splendid. I shall look forward to discovering the gardens."

Mrs Norton's gaze drifted back to Charlotte. "If you don't mind me saying so, Miss Fletcher, you look decidedly peaky. You are tired from your journey no doubt. There is an hour before dinner, so I suggest you have a little lie down."

They had begun to climb the stairs, but Lady Carstairs suddenly paused, her head cocked to one side.

"Is that a violin I can hear, Mrs Norton?"

"Yes, ma'am. Skelforth, our butler, practices for an hour every day. I should perhaps have told him of your arrival, but——"

"That is quite all right, Mrs Norton. I would

not have wished for him to be disturbed. I thoroughly approve of his endeavour."

If Charlotte's mood did not lift immediately, within a very few days, the many and varied efforts of her companions to amuse and distract her began to have their effect. Sir Horace continued her riding lessons and she was soon brave enough to venture into the park without being led, although she would not go anywhere near the river.

Sarah did not ride, however, even though Lord Seymore invited her. At first she claimed that she was too tired from the journey, and then insisted she could not leave Lady Carstairs unattended. But that eagle-eyed dame soon noticed this departure from her usual routine.

"Have you had a falling out with Lord Seymore?" she asked bluntly, as they sat in a sunny parlour, one morning.

Sarah glanced up quickly from the book of verse she had borrowed from the library. "No, ma'am, I have not."

"Then perhaps you will explain why you have not gone for your morning ride since we arrived?"

Sarah sighed. "Because I have indulged myself long enough. I must eventually return to the seminary and it will be easier to bear if I rid my-self of habits that I will have no opportunity to indulge there."

"I see," Lady Carstairs said. "Tell me, what poem is it that you are reading?"

Sarah glanced quickly down at the book in her hands and Lady Carstairs laughed.

"You have no idea, Miss Hayes, do not pre-tend that you do."

She gave a rueful smile. "You are right, ma'am. My mind was elsewhere."

"I am a good listener, Miss Hayes. And al-though you may find it difficult to believe, I can also be very discreet."

Sarah smiled. "It is not fair that you throw my own words back at me, ma'am."

"I never said I was fair."

As the smile faded from Sarah's lips, Lady Carstairs said, "Let me help you. You have dis-covered that Lord Seymore is not the man you thought him."

"Perhaps," Sarah conceded cautiously.

"I too thought he must be a selfish, scape-grace to have left Charlotte at the seminary all this time. But then I met you and realised it was perhaps the best thing he could have done."

"Thank you, ma'am."

"Shortly afterwards, I met Lord Seymore, and discovered there was rather more to him than meets the eye. He has a sense of humour and is not easily daunted for a start. In short, Miss Hayes, I discovered I liked him. Am I completely off the mark to suggest that you had a similar epiphany?"

"No, you would not be wrong," Sarah said quietly.

"And it has not completely passed me by that you have often seemed to enjoy each other's company."

"Yes," Sarah said simply. "I met him when I had my season and because of this shared history, I found I could talk to him about things… about my father. We were able to laugh together about memories I had all but forgotten."

Lady Carstairs smiled. "Laughter is very healing, is it not?"

"Yes," Sarah acknowledged. "But I am afraid I may have allowed my affections to become a little engaged."

"It was only natural that you should do so. But if he has not also done so, I am not as perspicacious as I like to think."

"I thought so too, ma'am. But I am afraid that we were both wrong."

"Nonsense. I do not believe it."

"Nevertheless, it is true," Sarah said with quiet certainty. "You see, when we were riding through the park at Priddleton, he told me that he had offered for a Miss Lucy Hopton, who is the daughter of the local magistrate, Sir Francis Hopton."

Lady Carstairs' jaw dropped and she was momentarily rendered speechless.

Sarah smiled wryly. "I must admit if we had not, the next moment, been distracted by Charlotte's scream, my reaction would have mirrored your own, ma'am."

They were interrupted by Skelforth. "Is Miss Fletcher at home to visitors?"

They exchanged a surprised look, for neither of them could imagine who might pay Charlotte a morning call.

"No," Sarah said. "She has gone riding with Sir Horace."

"Very well," the butler said, bowing slightly and turning towards the door.

"Wait!" Lady Carstairs said. "Who is it that wishes to see her?"

Skelforth turned back. "Miss Lucy Hopton, ma'am."

"Well do not keep her waiting. Show her in," Lady Carstairs demanded.

Not by a flicker did the butler display any

sign of displeasure at this less than gracious command; it had not taken him long to realise it was just Lady Carstairs' way. "As you wish, ma'am."

Sarah waited only for him to leave the room before rising swiftly to her feet. "I cannot stay, ma'am. You must see that."

"Sit down," Lady Carstairs said sharply. "I see nothing of the sort. Now I have had time to recover my wits, it occurs to me——"

What had occurred to her remained unspoken as Miss Hopton was just then announced. They exchanged polite nods and then she came towards Sarah, a friendly smile on her face.

"I am very pleased to make your acquaintance, Miss Hayes. Lord Seymore has often sung your praises." She turned to Lady Carstairs. "And I cannot tell you how very relieved he was, ma'am, when he discovered that you had invited Miss Fletcher to stay. He has always been quite hopeless where she is concerned, I am afraid. But I do not think we can, in all fairness, blame him, for she was a pitiful little thing when she came here, and he felt quite helpless. He never had any sisters you see. Of course, it would have been different if his mother were alive. She was such a gentle creature she would have been sure to draw her out. But all Jus… Lord Seymore's efforts proved useless, and gentlemen do so hate to be made uncomfortable, don't they?"

Sarah could quite see where her attraction lay. Her open, frank manners and clear humorous eyes were charming.

"How very true. Please sit down, Miss Hopton," she said politely.

"Thank you. Forgive me for rattling on like a veritable windbag. I met Miss Fletcher when she was last here and hoped to renew my acquaintance, not that I expect she will remember me."

"I am sure she will be very sorry to have missed you," Sarah said.

A short, awkward silence followed.

"I believe, Miss Hopton, that you have recently become engaged," Lady Carstairs said, in her usual direct manner.

Miss Hopton looked surprised and then amused. "Indeed I have, ma'am. But what can Lord Seymore be about to think you would be interested in the affairs of someone you have never met? I despair of him sometimes, really I do. This is unless… but no, you have lived in India so long, Lady Carstairs, and you, Miss Hayes, have been at the seminary, so it is highly unlikely."

"What is highly unlikely, Miss Hopton?"

Lady Carstairs said. "I have never thought my understanding to be at fault, but I am afraid you have quite lost me."

She laughed. "Oh dear. I quite see where your confusion lies. I was half talking to myself. What I had meant to say was that due to your individual circumstances, it was highly unlikely that you had met Mr Clayton."

Sarah's eyes snapped to Lady Carstairs. She could not fail to recognise the gleam of satisfaction that lurked in that lady's eyes.

"Mr Clayton?" she said, bemused. "But I thought Lord Seymore had offered for you."

Miss Hopton tilted her head a little to one side and gave Sarah a very direct look.

"He told you that?"

"Yes," Sarah said. "He most definitely said that he had offered for you."

Miss Hopton rolled her eyes. "And what else did he tell you, Miss Hayes?"

"Nothing, for we were interrupted at that point and have had no opportunity for private conversation since."

Of course it would have been more accurate to say that she had given him no such opportunity, but that would have revealed far too much of her own feelings, and Miss Hopton was, after all, a stranger.

"I see I shall have to explain," Miss Hopton said.

"I wish you would," Lady Carstairs said. "I suspected there might be more to this story than was immediately apparent."

"There is," Miss Hopton conceded. "It is true that Lord Seymore proposed to me. But his arm was twisted, first by my father, and then by me."

Sarah felt all at sea. "Yet you are engaged to marry Mr Clayton."

"Yes," she confirmed. "The thing is, my father and the late Lord Seymore were very good friends, and they both hoped we would make a match of it. When Mr Clayton asked for an interview with him, he sent for Lord Seymore on the flimsiest of pretexts. He tried to force his hand by giving him the impression that I wished him to offer for me, and all but persuaded me that he would be very cast down if I refused him. You must understand, Miss Hayes, that we are very old friends, and neither of us would wish to hurt the other. My father was, of course, quite aware of this."

"I have never agreed with arranged marriages," Lady Carstairs said disapprovingly.

"That is because for all your blunt, outspoken, and often rude manners, you are a hopeless romantic," Sarah said.

Miss Hopton looked from one to the other as if trying to gauge the nature of their relationship.

Lady Carstairs' lips twitched. "It is true, of course, but if you ever tell a soul I shall never forgive you." She turned back to Miss Hopton. "Am I to understand that Lord Seymore buckled under this pressure? I had not thought him so weak spirited."

"No, he did not buckle precisely. He asked me if I wished to marry him. I should have put him out of his misery at that point, for it was patently obvious to me, knowing him as well as I do, that he wished for the marriage no more than I did. I was extremely relieved, I assure you."

"Yet you did not put him out of his misery," Lady Carstairs mused. "Do you mind telling me why?"

Miss Fancot smiled. "No, not at all. It is not at all to my credit, but I could not help teasing him, just a little. But my main objective in wringing a proposal from him was to absolve him from all blame. It did not seem fair that my father's inevitable disappointment should be directed at his head when I had no intention of marrying him."

"Very noble of you, I'm sure," Lady Carstairs said. "But tell me, how did you *wring* a proposal out of him?"

"That was easy. We have always shared a good understanding, so I simply asked him to trust me and ask me."

Lady Carstairs gave a crack of laughter. "He must have trusted you greatly indeed to have put his head in your noose so tamely. He would have been in a fine pickle if you had accepted him."

Miss Hopton grinned. "He knew I would not serve him such a trick, besides, no female of any discernment would have accepted him." She sent a sideways glance in Sarah's direction. "His proposal was rushed and devoid of all feeling. I have told him to practice his address."

Lady Carstairs' eyes sharpened. "Was that because you feel he might need to make a more heartfelt attempt at some point in the near future?"

Miss Hopton rose to her feet. "As Lord Seymore has not indicated as much to me, I cannot say for certain, you understand, but I wouldn't be at all surprised if that proved to be the case. Now, I must take my leave, but I shall call again in the hope of catching Miss Fletcher at home."

"I like her," Lady Carstairs said as she left the room. "Very sensible sort of gal."

"Yes," Sarah murmured, distractedly smoothing one of the pages of the volume in her lap.

"I would not be at all surprised, if telling you he had offered for her was the preamble to a meandering and no doubt torturous proposal."

Uncertainty and indecision, leavened with a pinch of hope muddled Sarah's thinking. "Perhaps, I cannot tell. I am unsure of Lord Seymore's feelings, and I am not completely certain of my own."

"Do not go all missish on me, Miss Hayes, it does not suit you. If you do not care for him then why have you been avoiding him ever since you discovered he had offered for Miss Hopton?"

Sarah raised eyes that held a mixture of amusement and exasperation. "It is a pity females cannot enter the legal profession, ma'am. You share your husband's gift for incisive questioning."

"It is certainly important to have something in common with your husband, for no matter how attracted you are initially, that will only take you so far. I have seen more than one gentleman who was besotted with his wife when they married, fall rapidly out of love once he had slaked his thirst for her, and realised that she was an inane ninnyhammer for whom he had no use once she had provided him with an heir."

"I agree that attraction is not enough," Sarah said quietly. "But neither would I wish someone to offer for me out of gratitude or because they felt sorry for me."

"I wondered when your pride would rear its head again," Lady Carstairs said.

"It is not only my pride that makes me say so," Sarah protested. "Lord Seymore has expressed both of these sentiments on more than one occasion."

"A man don't always say what he is feeling, Miss Hayes. His actions often speak louder than his words. It seems to be that Lord Seymore has shown a marked predilection for your company. Has he given you no sign that his feelings are seriously engaged?"

A reminiscent smile curved her lips. "Well, he did knock Lord Turnbull down when he asked me to be his mistress."

"You did not tell me of this! The scoundrel! That is what comes of marrying without any affection at all! I feel very sorry for his wife."

"I am in agreement with you on that point, ma'am."

"It seems to me that if Lord Seymore was roused to such anger on your behalf, he must hold you in high regard."

"But he was not roused to anger, ma'am. He was very restrained. When Sir Horace thought that poor Mr Fancot had pushed Charlotte in the river, he hit him with fury, and then stood over him willing him to get up so he could do it again! Lord Seymore executed one clinical punch, and then calmly escorted me back to the ballroom."

She was not at all disappointed that Charlotte chose that moment to enter the room, for she felt they were getting nowhere. Her charge looked very pleased with herself and her eyes were sparkling.

"A letter has come for you Aunt Augusta," she said, handing the missive over.

"Thank you, my dear. Did you enjoy your ride?"

"Yes! I am finally getting the hang of it." She smiled proudly. "I managed a trot! I found it quite exhilarating."

Sarah laughed. "Wait until you try a canter! You will feel as if you are flying!"

"I shall look forward to it!"

Lady Carstairs had by now opened her letter and a small frown of concentration wrinkled her brow as she read it. Her grave expression sobered Charlotte.

"Is it from Uncle Oliver?"

"Yes, it is good news of a sort. Were you aware, my dear, that a person who is thought to have taken their own life cannot be buried in the churchyard?"

Charlotte gasped. "No, I was not."

"Do not alarm yourself, my love. That is what I meant when I said there was some good news. It appears that Doctor Smeathley had been treating Mrs Fancot for insomnia. He prescribed laudanum, but they had also discussed the merits of cherry laurel water as a sedative, although he deemed it too dangerous and advised against its use. He has taken the view that his patient decided to try it regardless, and has pronounced the death to be accidental."

"*Could* it have been accidental, Aunt?" Charlotte said, sombrely.

Lady Carstairs exchanged a brief look with Sarah, who gave a brief nod.

"Of course it could, my child. Mrs Fancot was very agitated and it is entirely possible that she took the water to calm herself. Because we knew her mind to be unbalanced, we may have jumped to the wrong conclusion."

Charlotte looked relieved. "Is my uncle coming soon?"

Lady Carstairs smiled. "The day after tomorrow."

CHAPTER 17

Lord Seymore sat at his desk lost in a brown study. It was not until Skelforth cleared his throat that he realised he was no longer alone.

"I have some letters for you, my lord," he said, shooting a close look at his master.

"Thank you, Skelforth, just drop them on the desk, will you?"

The butler glanced at the neglected pile of correspondence that already littered it. "I fear it would get lost, sir."

"Damn your impudence," he laughed, holding out his hand for the letters.

The merest hint of a smile disturbed the butler's countenance. "At the risk of incurring your displeasure further, may I ask if something is troubling you, sir? It is not like you to be so disorganised."

"The problem with servants who have known you since you were in short coats," Lord Seymore reflected, "is that they so often show a distressing lack of respect for one's privacy."

Skelforth bowed. "I would rather call it a proper concern for your welfare." He looked over his shoulder as he reached the door. "Perhaps there is something in the air, for when I took some refreshment to the parlour earlier, Miss Hayes also had a strangely distracted expression upon her face."

Lord Seymore frowned at the closed door for a moment and then sighed. It meant nothing. She was probably considering her next excuse for avoiding him. She had been cool towards him ever since the dreadful events of a few days ago, although he could not understand why. Perhaps she had been aware that he was about to propose to her and was at pains to ensure that he could find no opportunity to renew his efforts. He had been racking his brain to remember exactly what he had said to her, but everything before Charlotte's scream had become a bit of a blur. He glanced down at the two letters he still held, and opened the smaller of the two. It was little more than a hastily scribbled note.

Justin, you are an idiot! Miss Hayes has been labouring under the impression that we are to be wed. I have explained the situation as best I can; the rest is up to you. DO NOT make a mull of it. Lucy.

The fog in his brain suddenly cleared. He dropped his head into his hand and groaned. What a numbskull he was. He had told her that he had offered for Lucy, sure that she would appreciate the ridiculous nature of his proposal, but he had had no opportunity to describe it to her. He had meant to go on to explain why he had suddenly discovered he could not marry the woman he had thought to be his ideal match after all. He raised his head, a slow smile dawning. Her sudden withdrawal from him only made sense if Miss Hayes was not nearly as indifferent to him as she would like him to believe. He would take the first opportunity presented to him to bring this misunderstanding into the open.

He turned to his second letter. It was from Lord Carstairs. He gave a low whistle as he discovered how neatly he and the doctor had managed the affair. He pushed himself to his feet with renewed energy, and went to inform Mrs Norton to expect two more guests.

There was no immediate change in Miss Hayes' demeanour towards him. She replied politely enough to any comments he addressed to her at dinner, but made very little effort to hold up her end of the conversation. Her usual poise seemed to have deserted her and she was curiously reluctant to meet his eyes. However, this did not frustrate him as it had the evening before. Lucy's revelations appeared to have thrown her into some confusion, and although he was not completely confident of her regard, he was more hopeful than he had been before.

Lady Carstairs deigned to play for them that evening, leaving them very little opportunity for private conversation. Miss Hayes sat a little in front of him, and he contented himself with admiring the slender nape of her neck, the soft curve of her cheek, and the luscious promise of her lips. He was startled out of a very pleasant reverie, in which his own lips were trailing butterfly light kisses over the places his eyes had lingered, by the appreciative applause of the small audience. He hastily joined in, trying to make up for his tardiness with the enthusiasm of his clapping. The satirical glance Lady Carstairs sent in his direction suggested she knew exactly where his thoughts had been.

When the tea tray was brought in, Miss

Hayes poured. As she passed him his cup, her fingers brushed against his and the cup rattled in its saucer. Her eyes flew to his and her lips parted slightly.

"Thank you, Miss Hayes," he said softly. "Will you ride with me tomorrow?"

"Yes, Lord Seymore, I shall. Thank you."

He could not prevent the smile that curved his lips, and it widened as she turned from him and he caught Lady Carstairs' approving gaze and the sly wink she sent in his direction.

He went to bed more content than he had been for some days. He did not lay awake rehearsing what he would say; this time he would keep it short and sweet. That way there would be no room for any further misunderstanding between them.

He was an even tempered man, not given to sudden fits of temper or sullen moods, but he could have gnashed his teeth when he awoke to the unmistakeable sound of raindrops pattering against the window panes. He threw off his covers, strode across the room, and pulled the curtains back. Any hopes he had that it was a passing shower were instantly dashed. Roiling black storm clouds darkened the sky, promising a prolonged and heavy downpour.

He caught sight of his scowling countenance

in the window and suddenly laughed. He was behaving like a small child who had been denied a promised treat. He would clear the reports and correspondence that lay neglected on his desk this morning, and perhaps this afternoon he could persuade Miss Hayes to take a walk with him around the cloistered courtyard. It was not a very romantic setting, unless you delighted in all things gothic, but it would have to do.

Sarah did not spend such a comfortable night. Ominous rumbles of thunder frequently disturbed her rest. She tossed and turned, her mind a jumble of thoughts and images. The only man she had truly loved, was her father. Her heart had been torn to shreds when he died. She had felt somehow betrayed by him. And Lord Turnbull's actions had compounded that betrayal. The thought of bestowing her heart on another had been anathema to her. The seminary had been the next best thing to a nunnery.

But she was not a cold creature. Charlotte had become the receptacle for her affections. When she had seen her floundering in the river, she had felt a shard of ice pierce her heart, numbing it. Only when she had been sure that she had escaped a fever, had it begun to thaw. And then she had been surprised to discover how deeply the knowledge that Lord Seymore was to marry another had affected her.

Only the need to remove Charlotte from the scene of her recent nightmare had enabled her to face coming to Winbourne. When Miss Hopton had revealed that she was not engaged to marry Lord Seymore after all, she had felt stunned and unsettled, unsure if she wished to open herself again to possible pain and disappointment.

At dinner, Lord Seymore had gently teased Charlotte, telling her he had heard she had ridden her horse at a great wallop across the park, and Sarah had realised that he possessed the best qualities of the two previous men in her life. He loved his estate and his horses, as her father had done, but he was not a spendthrift, nor was he as reckless and mercurial in temperament. He had the looks and charm that Lord Turnbull had once possessed, but without the malice.

When her fingers had accidentally brushed against his that evening, her hand had trembled. When he had asked her to ride with him, his words had been like a softly uttered caress. Even if his affections were not as deeply engaged as her own, he had so much to offer her. The security he could offer was tempting, but his companionship and the prospect of remaining a part of Charlotte's life weighed far more heavily with her.

As the dark veil of night began to lift, she finally accepted that she loved him and would happily marry him if he should offer for her. And if he did not, she would savour each moment with him, and squirrel her memories away to sustain her through the dreary years that would follow. Her decision made, she fell into the deep, oblivious sleep of exhaustion.

By the time she came down to breakfast, Lord Seymore was just finishing his repast.

"Good morning, Miss Hayes," he said, rising to his feet and pulling out a chair for her.

"Thank you, sir," she said, smiling up at him. "I am afraid I overslept. The thunder kept me awake."

"You too, eh?" said Sir Horace. "Zeus did seem a bit annoyed last evening. I normally sleep like the dead, but even I woke a few times."

"I had not realised that you were a classical scholar," Lady Carstairs said, lifting a brow.

"I wouldn't call myself a scholar of any sort, ma'am," Sir Horace protested. "But I must say, you get some fine storms in Greece. They come from nowhere. One moment the sea is a tranquil pool, the next the clouds come racing across the sky, the wind begins to howl around the mountains, and all hell lets loose. It is a sight to behold, I assure you. If you are fortunate enough to be under cover, that is."

"I am a little afraid of storms," Charlotte said softly.

"No, no, you mustn't be," Sir Horace said. "There is nothing like being inside all snug and toasty, whilst the storm rages outside. The thing to do, Miss Fletcher, is to think of it as an errant child having a tantrum. The bolts of lightning represent him throwing his toys, the claps of thunder are his furious howls, and the incessant rain his angry tears."

Charlotte smiled. "You are very wise, Sir Horace."

Sarah and Lord Seymore exchanged a smile whilst Lady Carstairs was seized by a sudden fit of coughing.

"Oh dear, ma'am," Sir Horace said, concerned. "That don't sound at all healthy. I'd have a word with Mrs Norton if I were you; she's bound to have something that will soothe a cough."

Lord Seymore rose to his feet. "I am afraid that I will have to leave you all to your own devices this morning; I have some work I must attend to. Bamber, feel free to make use of my library, there are several volumes on classical Greece there, I believe. And ladies, please apply to Skelforth or Mrs Norton if there is anything that you require to keep you occupied."

The inclement weather kept them indoors all morning. After a light nuncheon, a fire was lit in the parlour and the curtains drawn against the lowering sky. Mrs Norton had uncovered Lady Seymore's old sewing box, and Charlotte applied herself to embroidering a handkerchief, Sarah browsed the volume of poetry that had failed to make any impression upon her the day before, and Lady Carstairs dozed by the fire. This domestic idyll was rudely disturbed when Sir Horace suddenly burst into the room, a large box in his arms.

"Brought some games to amuse you," he said cheerfully.

Charlotte hastily stowed her sewing in the basket, Sarah thankfully shut her book, having discovered it was filled with the sort of drivel that only the most sentimental of ladies might have enjoyed, and Lady Carstairs suddenly snorted, and sat bolt upright, her eyes snapping open.

"We were all very well amused, I thank you,

Sir Horace. There was no need for you to come blundering in like a bull in a china shop!"

"No, you can't have been, ma'am," he said surprised. "You wouldn't have been snor... that is sleeping, if you were."

Charlotte smothered a giggle.

"I was simply resting my eyes," Lady Carstairs said quellingly.

"What games are in there?" Charlotte said.

"Let's see shall we," Sir Horace said, sitting down and putting the box on the floor by his feet.

Charlotte knelt beside him, lifted the lid, and began pulling them out.

"Fox and geese," she murmured setting it aside. Next, she pulled out a pouch and emptied its contents onto the floor, a host of chess pieces scattered everywhere.

"Be careful, child," Lady Carstairs said. "There is nothing worse than looking forward to a game of chess only to find some of the pieces missing!"

Charlotte exchanged a smiling look with Sir Horace and they hastily collected them up. She pulled out another pouch and opened it more carefully.

"Spillikins!" she said, smiling. "I used to love playing it when I younger."

"You can play it at any age," Sir Horace promptly assured her. "As long as you've got nimble fingers."

They moved over to a table and emptied the ivory sticks onto it.

Lady Carstairs eyed Sarah speculatively. "I often enjoy a game of chess with Carstairs. I don't suppose you play, Miss Hayes?"

"As a matter of fact, I do," she said. "My father taught me to play. But it is many years since I have enjoyed a game. I will be a poor opponent, I fear."

"Then you must certainly practise," Lady Carstairs said firmly. "Is there a board to go with the pieces?"

Sarah delved into the box and found the desired object.

"Capital!" Lady Carstairs said, pulling an occasional table over to the fire.

She soon became so absorbed in the game that even the squeals of laughter that occasionally issued from the other side of the room, ceased to annoy her. She won the first two games, but the third was a close run thing. She sat back, satisfied.

"A few more games, Miss Hayes, and you will be a force to be reckoned with."

The door opened and Lord Seymore came

into the room. His brows rose slightly when he saw the chess set.

"Do not tell me that you disapprove of women playing the game?" Lady Carstairs said.

He laughed. "I would not dare, ma'am. Who was the victor?"

"I was on this occasion," Lady Carstairs said. "But now Miss Hayes has reacquainted herself with the game, I would not be at all surprised if that were not the case the next time we play."

She got to her feet and put her hands to the base of her back. "I have sat down too long. We all have."

A loud clap of thunder rattled the window, and even the curtains could not completely obscure the flash of lightning that swiftly followed.

Charlotte laughed. "That poor child is in quite a taking."

Sir Horace beamed proudly at her. "That's the spirit, Miss Fletcher."

Lord Seymore came a little further into the room, his eyes were fixed on Miss Hayes and so he did not see the sewing basket that sat by the chair. He stumbled slightly as he kicked it over.

"I say, old chap, easy does it," Sir Horace said, rushing over to pick up the odds and ends that had been spilled onto the floor. "You don't want to ruin Miss Fletcher's stitchery."

"Don't," Charlotte cried, as he bent and picked up the handkerchief she had been embroidering.

He stood a moment with it in his hand. She had embroidered his initials in each corner, and in the centre she had drawn a kingfisher, and had just begun to stitch its orange breast. His eyes rose to hers. "This is for me?"

"Yes," she said colouring. "But it is not yet finished. It is to thank you for… for coming to my rescue."

"Well," he said, puffing out his chest a little. "That's dashed kind of you. I shall carry it with me always, I can assure you."

"I hope you will not," Lady Carstairs said dryly. "At least not if you intend to use it!"

"I was about to go for a walk in the cloisters," Lord Seymore began.

"A splendid idea," Lady Carstairs chimed in. "We could all do with some exercise."

Another clap of thunder sounded overhead and she smiled. "I have an idea. Charlotte, we will put your mettle to the test, my dear. It seems to me that it would be a great shame to waste this splendid storm. Rather we should harness its atmosphere."

Charlotte looked a little uncertain. "How?"

"I wished you to learn to waltz, remember? This house stands on the foundations of a monastery. Beneath us is a cellarium. We shall ask Skelforth to put some candles in the sconces, I shall borrow his violin, and you shall all waltz. It will be like something from one of Mrs Radcliffe's novels."

"Do not tell me that you read them, ma'am?" Sarah said, surprised.

"And why not?" Lady Carstairs said. "I read a host of things. You never know what you will be called upon to discuss, after all."

"I hesitate to throw a damper on your scheme, ma'am," Lord Seymore said. "And as your host, it is my pleasure to afford you any amusement you might wish for, but I fear it may be a little cold down there."

"I was just coming to that," Lady Carstairs said, undaunted. "I suggest we all go and put something a little warmer on, and then meet back here in half an hour."

Lord Seymore was left with nothing to say.

As they traversed the cloisters, a strong gust of wind sent the rain slanting through the open arches that gave onto the courtyard. Sarah shivered and pulled her cloak a little tighter about her as they hurried to the huge oak door that was set in the wall at the end of the covered walkway. A series of steps led them down into a vast cellarium. Rows of columns supported a vaulted ceiling, creating a long series of arches that ran for at least a hundred feet. The draught from the door set the candles flickering. Eerie shadows danced on the columns, the effect magnified as a sheet of lightning lit up the windows set high in the walls.

"Magnificent," Sir Horace said. "I have rarely seen a finer example. I can almost hear the monks chanting!"

"Do not say so," Charlotte whispered, drawing a little closer to him. "Please tell me that no one is buried here."

"Of course there is not," he reassured her, leading her over to the rows of barrels and bottles lining the walls. "It is not a crypt. It was used much as it is today. It was nothing more than a storeroom, a cool place to keep the provisions."

"I can assure you, Miss Fletcher," Skelforth said, "That in all the years I have been coming down here, I have never heard or seen anything to cause me the least alarm."

He had set a chair for Lady Carstairs and his violin was set upon it.

"Where did you learn to play?" Lady

Carstairs asked, picking the instrument up and examining it.

"From my father, ma'am. He played in the church band. When he passed, he left his violin to me."

"It is very kind of you to allow me to borrow it," she said. "Now, I suggest that Miss Hayes and Lord Seymore demonstrate the steps. Observe them closely, Charlotte, and tell me when you think you are ready to attempt them."

She tucked the violin under her chin and drew the bow across the strings. As the first bright, clear notes filled the air, Lord Seymore held out his hand to Sarah. She smiled, a little self-consciously as she laid her own upon it, and allowed him to lead her beneath one of the arches. As he splayed his hand against her back and drew her to him, her lips parted as a soft sigh escaped her. Her eyes slowly rose to meet his and she became so lost in their midnight blue depths, that she was oblivious to the close scrutiny of her audience.

They began to move fluidly around the floor, gliding gracefully between and around the columns, the darkness occasionally brightened by another flash of lightning. The sound of the rain was drowned out by the hauntingly sweet music that filled the cavernous chamber. When it came to an end, they stayed a moment in each other's arms before the magical spell that had bound them was broken by the sound of clapping.

It was not their performance that had occasioned this show of appreciation, however. Skelforth's usually impassive countenance had become quite animated.

"Lady Carstairs, it is a privilege to listen to you. I only wish I was half so skilled."

She acknowledged his compliment with a gracious nod of her head. "You're ambition does you credit, Skelforth. I have had the leisure of many free hours to practise." She turned to Charlotte. "You did not stop me."

"I was enjoying watching the dance so much, you see," she said with a small smile.

"Yes, they do it very well. Do you have the steps now?"

"I think so," she said. "Although I doubt I will be able to perform the dance as elegantly as Miss Hayes."

"I would not expect you to."

Sir Horace turned and bowed to her. "Would you—"

"I suggest you partner Lord Seymore, Charlotte, and you, Sir Horace, take Miss Hayes. There will only be time for one more dance before it is time to dress for dinner."

CHAPTER 18

The storm dissipated sometime after dinner, and Sarah enjoyed a much more peaceful night than the one before. She fell asleep almost immediately, a small smile curving her lips. She slept long and deep and awoke long after the sun had risen. She sat up dismayed and rang for her maid.

"Frampton," she said frowning, "why did you not wake me? I told you I had intended to ride before breakfast."

"I did come in, miss, and I called your name but you did not stir. It seemed a shame to wake you when you were sleeping so soundly. But I did send a message down to the stables, ma'am."

"That is something, I suppose. I would not

like to have kept Lord Seymore waiting," she said pensively.

"No, ma'am," Frampton said, turning away with a knowing smile.

When she finally came down to breakfast, she saw his seat was vacant and felt a stab of disappointment.

"There you are, Miss Hayes, you are getting into very slovenly habits," Lady Carstairs said lightly.

"I know," she said, smiling ruefully.

"Coffee or chocolate, ma'am?" Skelforth asked her.

"Coffee please," she said, adding casually, "has Lord Seymore already breakfasted?"

"Yes, ma'am. He's had to go and visit one of our tenant farmers. A tree came down last night and has damaged his roof."

"I see."

"He is a conscientious landlord, as was his father before him."

"And what sort of a landlord are you, Sir Horace?" Lady Carstairs asked.

"I have a very good steward, ma'am. But I keep my hands on the reins, you may be sure. We take the wellbeing of our people very seriously."

"I am pleased to hear it," she said.

"My mother is also very interested in improving conditions for the poor souls who end up in the workhouse. I have visited several with her."

"That is very kind of you," Charlotte said gently.

"Visiting them is one thing, but how do you bring about any improvements?" Lady Carstairs asked.

"Donations," he said simply. "My mother is part of a committee which looks into these things. They have started a charity, and if an institution agrees to the changes recommended to them, they are provided with some support."

"I would like to meet your mother, I think," Lady Carstairs said.

"Bound to, ma'am. She is paying Loftus a visit, should have arrived by now."

"Then I shall look forward to making her acquaintance. Now, ladies, what say we visit Lymington today? I have decided to purchase some caps, and Mrs Norton assures me I will find some there."

"Caps?" Sarah said, surprised. She had seen Lady Carstairs wear nothing but turbans.

"Yes. I have decided it is time for a change. I thoroughly enjoyed my time in India, but one cannot live in the past, after all. It is time I embraced my new life."

"Very wise words, ma'am," Sir Horace said.

"Yes, well, when you interrupted my India day, my maid was extremely upset. I have discovered that she is not at all happy, and feel I was very selfish to bring her to England. I shall send her back, with a very good reference, and enough money to keep her comfortably until she can find another position."

They spent a very pleasant few hours in the town. Apart from a very pretty harbour surrounded by quaint cobbled lanes, it had a wide high street with a pleasing variety of shops. Lady Carstairs purchased a number of lace caps, a new bonnet for Charlotte, and a pair of gloves for Sarah, despite her protests that she had no need of them. They took some refreshment at one of the many inns, and returned to the house in the afternoon, very pleased with their day.

Sir Horace was strolling across the gardens as they pulled up in front of the house. He came up to them as they alighted from the carriage, a healthy glow in his cheeks and a bright gleam in his eyes.

"There are some fine walks to be had in this part of the country," he said. "I have had a very enjoyable few hours tramping about, and to top it all off, I spotted a white-tailed eagle. I hope your day has been as pleasant, ladies?"

"Indeed it has," Lady Carstairs said, "but I am quite worn out and would be grateful if you could contain your enthusiasm, Sir Horace, until we have at least revived ourselves with a sustaining cup of tea."

"Of course," he said, looking a little deflated. "Forgive me if I got a little carried away; it is not every day I see one, you see."

"I hope you will tell me all about it during our ride," Charlotte said gently.

"You are not too tired?" Sir Horace said, perking up.

Charlotte smiled. "Not at all. I shall run up and change immediately."

"Oh to be young again," Lady Carstairs murmured.

"You have more energy than many ladies half your age," Sarah said smiling, as Skelforth admitted them.

"That is hardly an accomplishment," Lady Carstairs said acidly, "when so many ladies these days appear to think that languid airs are all the rage and to drag themselves from their beds before nine, a feat to be admired!"

"You are harsh, ma'am," Sarah laughed.

"Perhaps," Lady Carstairs admitted. "But I

do so hate slothfulness." She turned to Skelforth. "I do not suppose Lord Carstairs has yet arrived?"

"No, ma'am. I do not expect him for another hour, at least."

"Perhaps I shall forgo my cup of tea and snatch a nap," she said, reflectively. "I would not like to appear jaded when he arrives."

"I shall have some tea sent up to your room, ma'am," Skelforth said, neatly solving her dilemma.

Sarah found herself at a loose end. She ran up to her room, shrugged herself out of her pelisse, and threw it rather carelessly over a chair, Like Charlotte, she was not at all fatigued by their jaunt into Lymington. After pacing up and down her room for a few minutes, she untied her bonnet, dropped it on her toilet table, and sat down. She looked into her mirror and tidied her hair. Her gaze shifted to the vase of flowers that graced the table. Her brows rose in surprise. Mrs Norton was usually so efficient, but the blooms were sadly wilted, and a few stray petals had fallen to the table. She rose and strode purposefully to the door. As she stepped onto the landing, she saw the housekeeper hurrying towards her, a harassed frown creasing her brow.

"Oh, Miss Hayes," she said, pulling up short. "Are your flowers drooping too?"

Sarah smiled. "Yes, a little."

"I do apologise," she said. "I was about to go into the garden to collect some fresh ones this morning, when Jenny, our maid of all work, took a tumble. I had to send for the doctor; her wrist was already so swollen, I knew she had broken it. No sooner had that been sorted, than Mary, our laundry maid, caught her finger in the mangle! Then cook discovered…" she paused and caught her breath. "Well, never mind. I do not know why I'm droning on about such things, but what with one thing and another, I have not managed to replace any of the flowers and we have more guests arriving at any moment."

"Mrs Norton," Sarah said gently, "if you will find me a basket, I will happily collect some for you. I am quite at a loose end, and I would enjoy it, I assure you."

"Well, if you're sure, ma'am, it would be most helpful."

The fragrant flower gardens soothed Sarah's restlessness. Soon her basket was full of roses, peonies, sweet peas, lilies, delphinium, and dahlias. The red damask roses were her favourite, and as she turned back towards the house she lifted one from the basket, closed her eyes, and held it to her nose, inhaling its fresh, bittersweet scent.

"Your beauty is more vibrant than any flower."

Her eyes flew open, she dropped the basket, and her fingers closed tightly on the stem of the rose as she watched Lord Seymore stride purposefully over the few feet of grass that still separated them. His face was serious and his chin, determined.

Wasting no time on pleasantries, he said, "I still have two questions which you have promised to answer truthfully, Miss Hayes."

Her heart beat a little faster. "I had forgotten our race."

"May I ask them?"

"Did I not say that I never renege on a wager?" she said softly.

He took a long slow breath. "Do you think you could be happy here?"

"Yes," she murmured.

He reached for her hand and frowned as he saw the bright red mark that stained her glove. Sarah had not felt the sting of the thorn as it pierced her skin. He stripped the glove from her hand, and a fresh bead of blood welled from her slender digit. Her eyes widened as he raised her hand to his lips and gently sucked the pad of her finger. He lowered it after a moment, but did not release it.

"Miss Hayes, it has been many days since I realised that the respect and gratitude I have long felt for you, had deepened into something far more profound," he said, his voice husky. "The indignities that you have suffered at the hands of persons so much your inferior, the humour and grace with which you have——"

He was silenced as she raised her hand and set her finger once more against his lips. She saw the sudden doubt that clouded his eyes, and said, "You made such a promising start. Trust me, and simply ask me."

Amusement chased the doubt away, and he grinned. "Miss Hayes——"

"Sarah," she said, smiling.

"Be quiet, woman!" he growled, pulling her into his arms.

"Oh, that I should suffer such indignity at your hands," she said woefully, "poor defenceless female that I am."

He silenced her with a long, lingering kiss. She melted against him, a quiver of desire running through her. When he at last raised his head, his eyes were darkened by passion, but a gentler emotion softened them as he raised both hands and cupped her face, brushing her lips with a feather light kiss.

"Sarah, I love you. Marry me."

"I must," she sighed, her gaze fixed on a point somewhere over his shoulder. "For I fear my reputation is quite in tatters."

He stepped away from her as Mrs Norton hurried up to them, hastily wiping away a tear. She made up for her unseemly show of emotion by her brusque tone.

"I wish you both happy, I'm sure, but I need those flowers, Miss Hayes. I have the vases lined up waiting, but they'll be wilting before I get the chance to arrange them at this rate."

Sarah passed the basket to her and the housekeeper smiled. "I couldn't have chosen better myself, ma'am. I shall have no qualms about handing this task over to you."

As she bustled away, Lord Seymore said, "I do have some qualms, however."

"You do not approve of my choice?"

"It is not your preference of flower that concerns me," he said pensively, "but the vases that house them. I must remember never to put you out of temper when there are any to hand."

Sarah laughed. "Or you could just make it an object with you, never to put me out of temper."

"I fear that will be impossible," he said gravely. "Now that you are forced to marry me, I will admit that I am a terrible pinch penny. I only spend money on my horses, and rarely visit Town more than twice a year."

"Then I see no need for any dissent between us, sir. I have no desire to visit Town, and I share your passion for horses," she said lightly.

She made no objection when he pulled her to him again, and reminded her of the other passion they shared.

"I will, of course, take you to London for the season," he said a little raggedly, some moments later.

"If you are thinking of Charlotte, then I will be happy to go, although I doubt it will prove necessary. But if you are thinking of me, there really is no need. It was my father's ambition that I cut a figure there. I much prefer the country."

"I am the luckiest dog alive," he said gruffly, lowering his head once more.

It was some time before they returned to the house. They entered by a side door and heard the unmistakeable sound of new arrivals. As they came into the hall, Lord Carstairs was handing his hat to Skelforth. A diminutive lady, with a kind face, and smiling hazel eyes stood beside him.

"Welcome, sir," Lord Seymore said, striding forwards to shake his hand. "I hope you did not find the journey too arduous."

"Not at all," he said. "We made very good time." He turned to Sarah. "You look very well, Miss Hayes. Allow me to introduce Lady Bamber."

That lady came forwards and took Sarah's hand. "I am so pleased to meet you, Miss Hayes. I feel I have much to thank you for. Loftus is full of your praises, you know. And I see he has not exaggerated one bit."

She smiled. "I really have done very little to deserve your thanks, ma'am."

"Yes, he said you were a modest creature, but if I find my son has changed even half as much as has been described to me, I shall be eternally grateful to you."

"My lady," Lord Carstairs said, strolling to the bottom of the stairs as his wife descended them. "That is a very fetching cap."

A delighted flush stole into that lady's cheeks. "What nonsense you do talk, Carstairs."

He took her hand and led her over to Lady Bamber, who smiled and said, "I must thank you for your kind hospitality to my son, ma'am."

"Please do not," she said. "He has proved useful in so many ways."

Lady Bamber looked a little surprised. "I am pleased to hear you say so. Where is he, I wonder?" she mused. "I find myself most impatient to see him."

"He took Miss Fletcher for a riding lesson," Lady Carstairs said. "I would have expected them to be back by now, however. But let us not stand about in the hall, come to the drawing room, ma'am. I am sure you would like some refreshment after such a long journey."

Skelforth went before them and opened the door. Lady Bamber's wish to see her son was instantly gratified. He stood in the middle of the room, Miss Fletcher clasped firmly in his arms, as he kissed her in a very thorough and unbrotherly fashion.

Skelforth cleared his throat and Sir Horace lifted his head, his eyes widening in alarm as he saw his audience. Charlotte gasped, colour rushing into her cheeks, and fled the room.

"Poor child," Lady Bamber said calmly, "she must be hideously embarrassed. I take it you have already proposed, Horace?"

"Of course, ma'am," he said, "I'm not a dashed loose-screw."

"I had not thought so," Lord Seymore said,

"but it occurs to me that you really ought to have asked my permission first, Bamber."

"I know I should," he said, frankly. "The thing is, we were practising our waltz—"

"I am fairly certain that when Miss Hayes and I demonstrated the dance to you, we did not kiss," he said dryly.

"You may as well have," Lady Carstairs interjected.

"I did not mean to kiss her," Sir Horace continued. "But she looked up at me, and her eyes were so… her lips were so…"

His mother came to his rescue. "I think we understand you, Horace." She turned to Lord Seymore, and smiled gently. "Please, do not tell me you object, for I would find the disappointment very hard to bear."

"I am not such a hypocrite, ma'am," he said, a wide smile crossing his face. "I have, not many minutes since, been caught in just such a compromising position with Miss Hayes."

"I knew it!" Lady Carstairs said, embracing Sarah. "I am sure you are now glad that I hid all your ugly, old clothes."

"It would not matter what Miss Hayes wore, ma'am," Lord Seymore said, "her quality would always shine through."

Lady Carstairs suddenly found herself in

need of a handkerchief, but the sudden tears that had sprung to her eyes blinded her, and she could not open her reticule.

"Here, my dear," Lord Carstairs said gently, passing her his.

"I am very happy for you, Miss Hayes," Lady Bamber said, her eyes twinkling. "I did for a moment wonder if perhaps you might be the very lady for Loftus, but it was clearly too much to hope for."

"I liked Mr Bamber very well," Sarah said, "but I do not think I would make a good vicar's wife. Now, I shall go to Charlotte."

"Yes, do," Lady Bamber said. "And bring her to me when she has regained her composure."

Sarah found Charlotte pacing her room, a little agitated, but by no means overcome.

"I do not know how I can show my face," she said.

"No one is the least bit shocked, I assure you," Sarah said, taking her hands. "Are you happy, my dear?"

"Oh yes," Charlotte breathed. "I only wish that you were as happy."

"Then your wish is granted," Sarah said softly. "I am to marry your cousin."

Charlotte threw her arms about her. "When

I saw you waltz, I knew you loved each other. I felt as if I should not be watching you, but I could not tear my eyes away!"

They returned to the drawing room, their arms around each other's waists.

"Come sit with me, Miss Fletcher," Lady Bamber said. "I wish to know everything, and I have some news that I think will make this day even happier for you."

Charlotte smiled shyly. "I do not think I could be happier, ma'am."

"Not even when I tell you that your good friend, Miss Montagu, is to marry Lord Cranbourne, who is our neighbour?"

"Oh, but that is wonderful!" Charlotte cried, sitting on the sofa beside her.

"Yes, I liked her immediately."

"And have you news of Lady Georgianna?"

"I only know that she has returned home," she said, retrieving a letter from her reticule. "Miss Montagu asked me to give you this, perhaps it will tell you more."

ABOUT THE AUTHOR

I love history and the Regency period in particular. I grew up on a diet of Jane Austen, Charlotte and Emily Bronte, and Georgette Heyer. Later, I put my love of reading to good use and gained a 1st class honours degree in literature.

I have been a teacher and tennis coach. I now write traditional Regency romance novels. I like to think my characters, though flawed, are likeable, strong, and true to the period. Writing has always been my dream and I am fortunate enough to have been able to realise that dream.

I live by the sea in Plymouth, England, with my partner, Dave. I like reading, sailing, wine, getting up early to watch the sunrise in summer, and long quiet evenings by the wood burner in our cabin on the cliffs in Cornwall in winter.

ACKNOWLEDGMENTS

Thank you Melanie Underwood for catching the things that fell through my net!

Thank you Dave for living all my books with me.